THE MIGHTY SHALL FALL

Raymond Parish

A Hank Anderson Novel:
Book 2

Copyright 2022

PRAISE FOR

THE MIGHTY SHALL FALL

"In *The Mighty Shall Fall,* therapist extraordinaire and amateur sleuth Hank Anderson—the male answer to Agatha Christie's Miss Marple—returns for another thrilling tale of misadventure—his insatiable curiosity, big-heart, and psychological savvy taking him down yet another dark rabbit hole."

— Mary Schanuel, co-author of *In the Moment: Writing from a Spacious Mind*

PRAISE FOR

OVERNIGHT DELIVERY

"*Overnight Delivery* is a refreshing mystery written by a new fictional author. The bulk of the storyline of *Overnight Delivery* takes place over a week...a very fast paced week. It added to the thrill of the mystery. It added to the climax of the story."

— Reader Views

"*Overnight Delivery* is an engrossing psychological thriller punctuated by wry humor and unexpected developments in a skillfully portrayed Iowa locale."

— Ron

"Raymond has sculpted a structured story cleverly and has made [*Overnight Delivery*] a compulsive read."

— Vijay M.R.

TITLES BY RAYMOND PARISH

Overnight Delivery

The Mighty Shall Fall

Copyright 2022 by Raymond Parish

All rights reserved. No part of this book may be used or reproduced by any means, graphic, electronic, or mechanical, including photocopying, recording, taping, or by any information storage retrieval system without the written permission of the publisher except in the case of brief quotations embodied in critical articles and reviews.

This is a work of fiction. Names, characters, places, and incidents are either the product of the author's imagination, or are used fictitiously. Any resemblance to actual persons, living or dead, events, or locales is coincidental.

The psychotherapy sessions as written in this book are not intended to be exact depictions of the therapy process, nor to resemble any actual sessions. They are fictitious approximations of psychotherapy utilized to create this work of fiction.

The font and formatting were set for readability.

Printed in the United States of America

To family, near and far.

Thanks to the fans of the Hank Anderson series.

If you read *Overnight Delivery* (if you haven't, please do) you know the teaser after **THE END** announced the next Hank Anderson novel as *Higher Education*, a prequel. Early in my work on the second book I realized I simply could not exclude several folks I had grown to love in the writing of *OD*, characters who would have been omitted in a prequel.

Haley. Jill.

Couldn't do it.

Welcome to the sequel.

There was no finer way to disappear. Red cedar Craftsman mansion topped with a charcoal gray corrugated roof. Interior exposed beams, cathedral ceilings, maple floors, and more windows than he had bothered to count.

The casual visitor, if there had ever been one, would have to climb the open three-tiered staircase to a $360°$ bonus room to get a panoramic view of the descending layers of landscape. Snowcapped mountains gave way to a tattered blanket of blue-green and burnt tan, evergreens battling to reclaim life from the onslaught of pine beetles, drought, and fire. Terraced aspens, soon to lose their leaves, flowed downward into expansive meadows, camouflage for gangs of ravenous elk in constant search of grass and the season's few remaining forbs. Bighorn sheep the color of dust merged with any and all terrain. Uninterested, the occasional moose commanded the shallows of a nearby wetland.

Most days, the only interruption to the arresting quiet outside his door was the early morning banter of scavenging magpies.

Countrified opulence. Purchased for a song from a Denver investment schmuck who thought time off the grid was a perfect post-divorce remedy for his high blood pressure. The seller failed to factor in a serious shortage of exclusive golf resorts, members only cigar bars, and younger women impressed by his money.

It was an easy sale. Cash deal. Bring enough ready money to the table and hard questions melted away.

The harsh echo of the man's smug, "sucker," was broken only by crackling softwood in a cultured stone fireplace taking the edge off the chill of the cavernous great room.

He swept his arm at eye level, as if capturing the horizon for an advertisement on Colorado tourism. Quite a step up from the Hole-in-the-Wall Gang's legendary refuge. He imagined Butch and Sundance would have understood that the real value of the place, luxury notwithstanding, was the seclusion. Even in full daylight this pretentious testimony to privilege and waste was nearly invisible, fused into the scarred magnificence of coarse red rock and dull granite. A crude entry road, little more than a well-worn trail, wandered over the narrow creek bed turned rambling river during spring thaw, only accessible by four-wheel drive in the best of weather.

Today did not look to become the best of weather.

In need of distraction, he let his thoughts drift to his favorite story, the contrast between this remote haven and the backwater hell he'd been born into.

His father had two full-time jobs after the machine shop laid him off. Fishing and drinking. Mom waited tables at the last diner in town with OPEN on the door, paying the rent and, until her husband fell in the river and lost the keys to the only reliable family truck, investing far too often in the local DUI lawyer's vacation home. His older brother enlisted in the army to get away. Sporadic emails hadn't recommended a steady diet of triple digit heat mixed with frequent gunfire as a profession.

He didn't run away from home that oppressively humid day in mid-August. He simply packed his frayed dollar store gym bag full of worn blue jeans, thrash metal t-shirts, and a tattered copy of The Art of the Deal, walked to the washed-out welcome billboard at the town limits, and put his thumb out for the first ride west. He was 17. One year short of legal in Missouri. Old enough to leave when nobody cared enough to track you down.

It had been twenty-two years since the last long-haul trucker dropped him in downtown Denver, alongside the other unseen street people. He clawed his way uphill, never using his given name, ridding himself of his 'Missoura' accent. No drugs. No friends. No arrests. No shelters or social workers. Working the streets. Staying mobile. Changing cities often. Perfecting his craft.

He taught himself about the one-percenters, the rich and powerful, not the bikers, learning how to dress himself from men's magazines in the library. He rotated from branch to branch through the seasons, sitting in a corner until closing time, loving the quiet hum of the AC in summer, or the heat that restored feeling to his hands and feet on nights of piercing cold.

He read classic literature. Taught himself to use their computers. Studied banking. He even learned to cut his own hair.

After years of petty preying on the privileged—he loved his catchphrase—with practiced invisibility, having built a stockpile of accessible cash, he moved into management. A small crew. Kids with stories like his own. Hungry. Smart. Willing to take big risks.

His band of dreamers.

These days, each of them had a stash. More than enough money to live in comfort. For now. But not enough for a "get the hell out of the country before our string of wins runs out and the law catches up with us" retirement plan. In any event, comfort was to his mind synonymous with a slow march back into the living hell of an ordinary life.

The time had arrived for a new dream. Five years of planning. A year of successful dry runs. Fine-tuning. Prep for the grand finale.

Hazardous? No danger, no high. Brilliant? Absolutely.

His face burst forth with the lacquered-on smile of a TV evangelist. He had risen like the Phoenix in the Greek myths he consumed during the lean years, emerging from the ashes of his austere beginnings to the triumph of his future vision.

A rush of blood to his center, triggered by the love of his singular genius, drew him back to the moment. He stared through the wall of windows at Long's Peak. Feathery sheets of cirrus clouds cloaked the mountain range to the west, blocking any promise of sun, advance warning of a serious early season storm gathering speed and moving his way. Turning toward the barnwood table in the center of a kitchen that looked like a tribute to stainless steel, he willed the idle laptop to chime, wondering if a pop-up blizzard was destined to vaporize his already dicey connection to the outside world, forcing him to abandon his sanctuary ahead of schedule.

Contingencies. He was accustomed to minor hiccups. Plan, then adapt. If needed, he had a lesser safe house with better reception.

But the kid was more than a hiccup.

Staring into the bottom of the empty tumbler in his hand, the feel-good energy coursing through him was dislodged by his only sworn enemy, a surge of indecision that could derail reasoned thought and release a torrent of self-doubt into the pit that occupied the core of his being.

A third round of rich Woodford Reserve sipping bourbon wrestled the beast into submission. The elixir restored his belief in his natural superiority and the suppleness of the plan. He sat. Enveloped by the billowing softness of the cowhide sofa, he closed his eyes, the snap of embers a lone disruption to the night closing in.

He woke, disoriented and sluggish, his dreams invaded by marbles of sleet scatter-gunning against the window glass. The fire was dead and a darkness with no apparent beginning or end had come over the mountains. The luminous dial of his Rolex gave off an oozing blue light, a pronouncement that he had slept well past the designated time for the download. Angered by the delay, he stood too quickly and rocked on his heels, the jolt bringing tears to his eyes. Pressing a hand to his forehead, he cursed the lie that expensive booze didn't cause hangovers.

The warning blast of bitter wind slapped his back a fraction ahead of his dulled defense system.

He didn't feel the crushing blow. His special world simply went away.

WEDNESDAY

My counseling practice wasn't exactly booming. The cliché—due to no fault of mine.

Not so in my case. Almost two years beyond what my business partner, Dennis Greenberg, and I dubbed, The Mess in the Fall, I was still navigating the path of destruction left behind by the tragic life and death of Kenny Jensen. I worked enough to stay solvent and meet my commitments to Anderson & Greenberg Counseling. I continued to spend as much time as possible with my daughter, Haley, in the increasingly busy schedule of another high-octane Anderson. I had also renewed my passion for cycling, medicine for the mind, body, and spirit. And maybe, a form of avoidance.

I was checking the spin on the tires of my more speeds than I'd ever need Trek touring bike when Belinda's text pinged.

Call me.

My distaste for technology is well known among associates and friends. Belinda is unmoved by this, regularly sending texts my way. I dialed the office.

"Anderson & Greenberg Counseling Associates. This is Belinda."

"I'll be in this afternoon."

"Good morning to you, too, Hank. You have a little more than an hour to get here to meet your new client."

Belinda Clark, our office manager and my self-appointed life coach, believes she channels my deceased mother and is charged with, as she so colorfully explains, "keeping your damn self somewhere near this side of the line."

"The phone rang as soon as I got in the office this morning," she said. The caller, male, handed the phone to another man, who told her he needed to see Hank Anderson about problems in his life. Judging I had far too much free time on my hands, Belinda assigned him a same day intake appointment.

"Don't you think it would have been better to call me first? You know, check to see if I had other important plans."

"You mean like putting on those silly looking shorts and riding your over-priced bicycle instead of working to pay your bills and feed your family?"

Busted.

"That's harsh." My response conflicted with my internal dialogue.

"I stopped at Smokey Row for coffee and scones on my way in today, hotshot." I could feel the warmth of her smile through the connection. "In case you don't have time to pick something up before you get yourself to work."

"I'll be there shortly." I parked my bike back in the garage. "Thank you."

"We have to look out for one another, Hank," she said. "That's what we do."

Avoidance issue resolved for now, I swapped my cycling suit for a white on gray pullover, black jeans and my favorite black suede loafers, grabbed a fistful of keys, and pointed my trusty Jeep north, then east. Idling at the light on Ingersoll, I checked out the Des Moines skyline, dominated by the high-rise insurance trade buildings overlooking our extraordinary Pappajohn Sculpture Park—unrelated to the pizza empire. Further east, I caught a glimpse of the State Capitol gold dome, Iowa's overstated beacon for shading the truth and outright lies. An old friend, curiosity, drew me into wondering about my new client. I was pulled back by the blast of the horn from a local produce truck on my bumper, telling me the light had gone green. I gave a thumbs up in the mirror and motored on.

On the half-hour, I stood in our outer office, blueberry scone resting comfortably in my belly, reheated cup of coffee in hand. I attempted eye contact with someone Dad would call, "rail thin." He was a disheveled, bare-foot young man, sitting in an armchair in the lotus position, a distant frown set into his cherub-like face. Soft brown hair flowed past his shoulders. He was dressed like a peasant from one of those ethnically careless 'Spaghetti

Westerns' my uncle loved, the ones that gave Clint Eastwood his ultra-violent white man start. More boy than man in appearance, my new client's delicate features suggested startled innocence as a first impression, flawed by shocking half-circles of fatigue under each eye.

I read his sparse client demographics sheet. Name: Seth Oberstreet. Age: 19. Signatures for consent for services and consultation. No details. Lots of blank spaces. Cash for the session pinned under the clipboard.

"Seth?"

He looked up, aware of my question but no less distant.

"Yes, sir."

"I'm Hank Anderson," I said, pointing to my office. "I'll be meeting with you."

"Okay." He stood and followed me without question, resuming his cross-legged position in a winged-back chair at the far corner. It provided plenty of space from the maroon leather chair and up-scale cherrywood desk I relied on to temper my memory of a past break-in. The vile graffiti still lurked beneath repainted walls.

I leaned back in my chair.

Plenty of distance. Safe container.

"I didn't see anyone in the waiting room with you, Seth." Casual opening. Another man dialed the phone that led this young fellow to me.

"Lawrence drove me from the camp and dropped me off. He said he'd come back."

"You live in a camp?" I kept the surprise out of my question.

"I've been there for a while." Something in his eyes told me it was too soon to ask—for how long?

"Can you tell me who Lawrence is?"

"He's the leader of the group at the camp." Specific questions, specific answers. I pretended to write something important on a legal pad to buy time, then smiled an invitation into further discussion.

"What brings you to see me today?"

"Lawrence told me it would be good to see a doctor. I'm having bad dreams." He squinted to read the framed diplomas on my wall. "Are you a doctor?"

"I'm not. I'm a psychotherapist. Some people call me a counselor."

His question was replaced by a shrug.

"You seem nice." His frown deepened. "I really don't like those dreams."

Here we go.

"What are your dreams?"

Seth unfolded his legs and leaned in, as if attempting to penetrate a dense fog.

"I love everybody at the camp. There are so many special people. We sing, we meditate, we share food, we work. It's peaceful." He retreated, pulling his feet to the chair cushion. "I don't understand why I wake up at night."

"You're having trouble sleeping?"

He hid his face between his knees. "Yes."

Repeat.

"What wakes you up, Seth?" He raised his head and looked through me, dismay creasing his smooth skin. "I think I'm going to have to hurt them. And run away."

In the work I do, I've seen a long line of faces struggling with unsolvable puzzles.

"It doesn't make sense," he said. "We're friends. We love each other."

Seth and I spent the next hour in a painstaking effort to divine the origins and depths of his disturbance. He was not specific about any harm he had considered for those at the camp. He had no concrete plan or intent. He was holding on dearly to one morsel of clarity. The nightmares plaguing his sleep were completely incongruent with the person he knew himself to be.

"I've never even been in a fight."

We required a round of wandering conversation to establish that Seth did know he was somewhere in Iowa. When I told him our offices were in Des Moines, he turned to my window, as if he might spot the camp, which was "a bit of a drive from here."

He was also clear on the circumstances that brought him to this strange land. An only child, his parents owned a successful construction company in southwestern Colorado. An uncertain number of weeks ago he'd been struggling through the second semester of his freshman year of college, lost in the white-water rapids of the university experience.

"I'm the quiet one in the family."

I waited. His eyes indicated maximum effort toward collecting a sequence of events.

"I made it through the first semester. The classes were easy. The people were nice."

But.

His delicate complexion reddened.

Embarrassed.

"But I mostly studied and did stuff with video games in my room."

An introverted kid away from home for the first time.

I recalled an extroverted kid away from home for the first time.

I mostly squeaked through classes and partied.

"Do you like video games, Mr. Anderson?" There was a flicker of enthusiasm in his voice.

"I'm more of a library guy."

"Libraries are good." His tone suggested he was awake enough to decide I was from some bygone pre-tech culture. "What were we talking about?"

"Challenges at school."

"Yeah. Yeah. I've been forgetting things." He tapped his temple. "My parents thought I should move back home and take a semester at the college in town where my high school friends go. Be around people I know. Take the pressure off."

But.

"But I was determined." He planted his feet on the carpet. "When I got back to campus after holiday break, I started studying in the Student Union. To be around other people. I tried to pretend I was like my mom." He managed a slender smile. "She has about a thousand best friends."

His smile flat-lined. "But I'm not my mom. One day, Lawrence came up and asked if he could sit with me. He said I looked lonely. I told him I was. He invited me to a group meeting he started to help young people find their center and connect with other students. I didn't know what finding your center meant, but he was so easy to talk to." His eyelids fluttered, as if soothed by the memory. "I didn't have anything else to do, Mr. Anderson."

"So, you went to the meeting."

"I did. It was great."

From Seth's description of the days that followed, I determined one meeting led to a series of weekly gatherings. The group content sounded like a jumble of intro to metaphysics, overly simplistic mindfulness exercises, and a readymade friendship experience for socially awkward young folks. Not exactly cutting-edge stuff, but it worked for Seth.

"Contessa. Cyril. Harold. Meg." He wrapped his arms around himself. "We all got along."

Give him some breathing space.

I sat back and pretended to check my notes. So far, there was little to set off my internal warning light.

Except.

At the center of each experience was the man called Lawrence—no last name—introducing them to The Scholars of Calm. He opened every meeting with a quote from its founder, Tyr Taranis, who pronounced the organization to be, as quoted by Seth, "a student movement committed to fostering inner and world peace on a growing number of campuses across the Great Plains."

Lawrence. Single names only are for musicians, deities, and creeps.

After several months of group get-togethers, with summer term well under way, Seth and his newfound pals were encouraged to join students from other campuses for a multi-week national conference at a rustic retreat center in the Midwest.

"Mom and Dad are very protective, Mr. Anderson. They were happy I made friends, but they wanted me to come home for the break."

In another well-intentioned effort to exert his independence, Seth garnered the reluctant support of his parents and ponied up a substantial registration fee from his personal account. A two-day extended road trip with Lawrence later, he and several of his new friends found themselves in the middle of a state he had previously only seen from the window of a commercial jet flying east for family vacations.

"Levi, Emma, and Theodore were representatives from other schools."

Were?

He shrunk deeper into the chair, his look morphing to child-like alarm. "It was good until Levi was cast out for falling asleep during meditation time. Lawrence said we should love him, but he was not ready to be an agent of change. Since he left, I've been waking up before the allotted 4 hours."

Cast out?

"Lawrence says guided sleep and simple food opens our hearts and minds," he added. "But, I'm pretty tired. And hungry."

I wrote FOUR HOURS and AGENT OF CHANGE on my legal pad.

While Seth answered my follow up questions about his daily routine, I multi-tasked, beginning to cobble together the nuggets of his distress. It was clear he was suffering from deprivation: lack of sleep, poor nutrition, and a high level of physical exertion in the form of many hours in the camp's garden. For good measure, attendees spent evenings in "community building"—a round robin of members hammering home the philosophy of the movement through poetry and songs.

"Can you give me an example, Seth?"

He pulled a laminated card from his pocket and read to me:

> **We are The Scholars of Calm.**
> **We are seekers of peace.**
> **We are The Scholars of Calm.**
> **We are agents of change.**
> **We are The Scholars of Calm.**
> **We are one with calm.**
> **We are one with calm.**
> **We are one with calm.**
> **We are one with calm.**
> **We are The Scholars of Calm.**

He held the card up, like show and tell. "He's on his way to celebrate with us at the close of the conference, Mr. Anderson." His head sunk back to his knees. "But, Levi won't get to meet him."

"Who's on his way?"

"Tyr Taranis."

"When will that be?"

He looked up. His face registered the frustration of a student given a test question not covered in the class material. "Lawrence hasn't told us."

I made sure the uptick in my pulse rate wasn't reflected on my face. The signs of what Seth had fallen victim to were becoming more clear. Already in the throes of deprivation, perhaps indoctrination, Levi's dismissal from the group had tipped his emotional scales, taking him to the edge of his compromised physical and mental state.

Who the hell are these people?

A calmer voice in my head intervened.

Relaxed concern.

"Have you spoken to your parents recently?"

"I called home right before we got to the camp. We all made a pledge to give up our devices while we're here. To remove distractions and fully engage in our process." He sounded like he was reciting from the brochure. "Lawrence let us write letters to tell our families we were doing well. He mailed them for us."

Let you.

"I miss my mom and dad."

Isolate from family.

"Of course you do."

Time to step up.

"Seth, I appreciate how open you've been, especially when you're so tired. I'd like to offer you a couple of thoughts."

"Sure."

"Any of us can get confused if we don't get enough sleep for weeks in a row," I started.

He nodded and moved to his feet. "Lawrence told me you would give me something to help me feel better. I do. I'll tell him I need more sleep. Thanks for the advice." He moved toward the door as if we'd solved the riddle.

Keep up.

"Seth." I stood slowly, giving him space.

What are these people planning? Why would they send him to me? Smile.

"I think it would be good if we asked Lawrence to join us when he comes to pick you up."

"Okay." Compliance was the clear mantra of this group's doctrine. "But, can we go outside and wait? I'm not used to being indoors this much." He cast a nervous glance, as if noticing the closed space for the first time.

"Definitely." I pulled a business card from the tray on my desk. "Can I trade you one of my cards for the poem you read?"

He laid the reading on the desk and dropped my card in his pocket. I retrieved my cell phone and led him toward the exit, pausing to get Belinda's attention.

"Belinda, Seth and I are going to wait for his ride. Can you give Phil Evans a call and tell him I need to move our meeting up? It would be great if he could call me on my cell as soon as possible."

Her smile didn't reach the question marks in her eyes, but she got on board. "Right away, Hank. Nice to meet you, Seth."

"You, too, ma'am."

I avoided the enclosure of the elevator. We took the stairs to the lobby. Seth's gaze lingered on the drink machine.

"Can I get you a drink? There's soda and water."

"I haven't had a soda for a long time, Mr. Anderson. A root beer would be nice."

"A favorite of mine, too. Root beer, it is. And you can call me Hank."

He hesitated, as if any informality might be a breach of protocol. "Thank you."

I found my ever-present stash of pocket cash and fed some into the slot. In sync with the clank of the beverage release button, a gust of autumn air warmed the back of my neck. Over my shoulder, the lobby door eased closed. Seth was on the other side. He walked to a weather-beaten red pickup truck with rusted wheel wells, opened the passenger door, hesitated, and climbed in. With the sun shimmering off the glass, the driver was no more than a silhouette. The truck stuttered into a U-turn with the sound of a muffler near its end times.

Root beer in hand, I got out the door in time to see the driver take a left onto Ingersoll, gaining speed toward the city. I caught a partial on the license, WK, as they blended into traffic and disappeared. The colors on the plate, green and white, were not of Iowa vintage. Resisting the urge to run after them, with no better option in mind, I popped open the root beer and trudged back up the stairs.

This is bad.

Belinda was ready for me. "Phil didn't pick up. I left him a message, but he hasn't called back yet."

"Let me know as soon as he does," I said. "Thanks."

I got to my office and closed the door before she could demand further information, pretending to work on my new file. I stared at Seth's near empty data sheet, kicking myself for not getting his parents' phone numbers and scouring my brain for any magic that would allow me to manifest his location and race to his rescue. My startle reflex discharged when Belinda knocked and barged through my door.

"It's Phil, on Line 2. You must be very worried about this Seth." She closed the door behind her.

"Thanks for getting back to me, Phil."

"What's wrong? We don't have a meeting scheduled."

A reasonable question. Detective Phil Evans and I had history that included the DEA, street dealers, and multiple deaths. We'd taken a break from sharing cases.

Today, I needed him.

I gave him an abridged account of my extended intake with Seth. I feared the young man could continue to decompensate and, although the danger was not imminent, become a risk to himself or others. Believing the greatest threat to his well-being was his return to the camp, I closed the deal by reading Phil the laminated card Seth left with me.

Phil could do phone silence as well as he did in-person silence.

"Detective?"

His response had a timbre similar to the old truck's muffler. "Lawrence. The Scholars of Calm."

My gut butterfly flapped double-time. "Yes."

"We're not sure how long these people have been around. They've kept a low profile. A report was passed down about a call from a convenience store in Ankeny. The owner said two, quote, weirdo hippies came in for supplies last week. He overheard the name of the man who acted like he was in charge. Lawrence. They didn't do anything illegal. The owner just didn't like them."

"Outdated reference to hippies aside, he might have been on to something," I said.

"What do you need?"

"A Des Moines Police Department wellness check."

"How about a joint police and mental health professional wellness check?"

Last year, Phil and I attended a workshop on active collaboration between law enforcement and mental health providers.

"If the captain clears this, you and I could take a ride tomorrow morning." Phil was a stickler for chain of command. "You're the evaluating mental health professional. It's appropriate for you to re-assess Seth in his current environment."

"It would be better to go now."

"It would be if we knew where to find him. I need time to establish their location."

"Point taken."

Belinda knocked softly and stuck her head in. "Your next client is here."

Phil promised to call if he found The Scholars of Calm before nightfall. If I didn't hear from him, we'd meet the next morning at what my dad calls, "the crack of dawn."

~~~

In therapy, the outside world can disappear for a period of time. Everything that matters is contained within the four walls of the office. One popular phrase—being fully present. My preference is Csikszentmihalyi's concept of Flow, being completely absorbed in an activity of value and challenge. I had once read he compared this to jazz improv. In the beginning, my work with Terrence was more like grinding it out in irregular meter than playing inspired jazz.

Seeking help was far removed from the masculine imperatives he'd been raised to believe in, such as, real men solve their own problems. His younger sister identified a flaw in his logic.

"I love you brother." His imitation of her shrill voice pecking at the edges of his resistance was a privilege given only to siblings. "I will listen to you anytime, but I am not a professional and this nervousness you wake up with every day is serious stuff. Strong and stubborn are not the same thing."

The sister's compassionate confrontation became the impetus the man needed to show up. Naming the monster that stalked him took longer. He used up several sessions with thinly veiled doubts about my experience, knowledge, and the height requirement for first-tier psychotherapists before arriving at his no-nonsense self-assessment.

"A constant fear of failure."

Not the kind of fear that causes a less than stellar day, or makes a person avoid a dark alley at night. This was a beast that lurked constant, in the shadows, showing up in sleepless nights, heart palpitations, tremors, and cold sweats engulfing Terrence's entire body. A fear not based in fact, but in the two-choice method of defining success: perfection or failure.

At our next session, he came in with the story of the trigger mechanism for these debilitating anxiety attacks.

Terrence was an exceptional athlete from northwest Iowa. Recruited to South Dakota, he'd been an All-American on his university track team. He was now the track coach and algebra teacher at a 3A high school just past the Des Moines city limits. I estimated the span of his running stride was about equal to the length of my entire body.

"Let me ask you a question, Hank."

"Absolutely."

"Is there anything you had a special talent for as a kid?"

"You mean other than getting in trouble?"

"Yeah." He could tell I wasn't joking. "Other than getting in trouble."

"I could remember stories people told me better than anyone else I knew. At the time, not a marketable skill."

"Did anyone ever say, this kid has a great memory for stories?"

"No."

"I loved to run. I remember the first time I heard, this boy is really fast. Seven years old. I was winning races against the high school kids by the time I was in junior high. My parents were great. But the faster I got, the hotter the spotlight got. People were talking about the Olympics when I was sixteen. Old racists telling me I was going to be the next Jim Thorpe."

He stood and paced the room, waiting to hear if I recognized the name.

"Jim Thorpe. Maybe the greatest all-around U.S athlete, not only Native American athlete, of all times. Robbed of his Olympic medals by a committee of people that didn't follow the rules they made. His medals were reinstated years after his death."

He sat. "Right."

"A lot of pressure for a kid running fast and having a good time."

"Exactly. The fun ended. I don't know what they call stage fright for runners, but I caught whatever it is. Sweats, nerves, doubt. I still hold conference records in high school and college, but I choked at the nationals. I had meltdowns before both of my events. I was lucky to finish." His shoulders sagged into the memory of that day. "I sweat through two shirts before my first interview at the high school. Math is for serious people. I told myself I got the job because of my track resume, not my interview skills or intelligence. More luck."

His expression was not one of a man who felt lucky. "How am I supposed to teach kids when I can't keep my own self together?"

By the time he rescheduled, we had decided to put our combined efforts into answering his question.

Today, two months down the therapeutic road, Terrence carried himself like a man on a trajectory to win his next race. He'd begun to practice an immediate response system of breathwork and internal dialogue to regulate his anxiety in moments of rapid onset. He'd incorporated meditation into a familiar routine of solitary physical training. On a more fundamental level, he was pulling apart his definitions of success, manhood, and courage in the context of a world beyond my grasp. He could now see how his progress would enhance his ability to encourage and challenge athletes and math students as a coach and teacher.

When we closed out our work for the day, Terrence stood and looked down from his superior point of elevation.

"All due respect, Hank, you are large in spirit, but short of body. And very white."

"All due respect, Terrence, that is not an observation of which I am unaware."

"A poor effort at humor," he said. "I'll give it another go. Our life experiences are worlds apart. There are things about me you cannot possibly understand."

Wait.

"But, you helped me get out of my own way. That's what good coaches do. That's why this therapy stuff works for me."

Terrence gave Belinda a wave on his way out the door. I followed his graceful exit, allowing myself a few steps to reflect on his evaluation.

"Terrence is looking good, all-star."

"He's doing the hard work."

"You're still lousy at false humility." Her adulation was brief. She wanted answers. "No messages, Hank. What is going on with your new client?"

"I'm more than a little worried. He left without any follow up scheduled. Phil and I are going to visit him where he lives tomorrow. A wellness check."

Smile to affect a casual demeanor.

She returned her own, more nervous smile, its origins based in considerable knowledge of my long-standing tendency to act now and think later. "Oh goodness. I set up the intake. Did I get us in a bad situation?"

Us.

"No." I pretended I knew the answer. "You'll be pleased to know I've done my due diligence." She also kept a complete record of my previous excursions into dangerous corners of the world. "I called for backup."

"Well, as long as you're not going off willy-nilly on your own and the detective is in charge, I give you permission to go." We both pretended she could have stopped me. "You don't have any clients scheduled for tomorrow, but you have people on Friday."

She stood and slipped into her famous designer whose name I wouldn't recognize silk jacket. Belinda and her husband, Cal, invested well and she doesn't need the modest income provided by Anderson & Greenberg Counseling to, as Dad says, "dress to the nines." When Cal died unexpectedly five years ago, she filled some of the space left by the love of her life with grandchildren, friends, and her role as my primary advisor in all things professional and personal. Office manager, life consultant, non-bio aunt to my daughter. She does it all.

"I'm off to Valley Junction to meet the women from my reading group."

I looked at the wall clock.

Damn.

I grabbed my canvas briefcase and escorted her to her latest new car, a pearl white Tesla. The engine booted up without a sound. She motored away in search of 5th Street south at the speed of a combine moseying down a two-lane road to a distant corn field. None of the following traffic honked. I assumed everyone knew her and were afraid of the repercussions.

In contrast, I jumped in the Jeep and hit the stereo play button on My Morning Jacket. I'd read that car companies were eliminating CD players from all new vehicles. I turned the volume up to drive the absurdity from my head, with a vow to keep my blue machine running for another hundred thousand miles. I cheated on the speed limit in familiar fashion and covered the backstreets in less than 30 minutes, pulling up to the quaint house built in the style locals call— Beaverdale Brick. I no longer called it home.

My old school wristwatch said no minutes to spare. I hustled up the concrete porch steps.

Made it.

The door was yanked open by the fourth grader who used to be my little girl, a constantly growing version of the woman behind her. These days, I actively avoided any review of my dazzling ex-wife's curves.

"Hey there. I didn't see the car in the drive."

Brilliant.

"Car's in the shop, Dad. Mom got a ride home from Milly. I've been ready for like a half hour." Haley's disapproval had a familiar ring. "I don't want to be late and I'm hungry. Everybody's going to be at Kelli's early tonight. We're working on a project."

Gail was classy enough to blush. "Come in," she said. "You have plenty of time, Haley."

I stepped into the entryway and clicked the latch, with Mom in my head yelling, "Close the door, do you live in a barn?" Dad is the master of aphorisms, but Mom had her moments.

"Get your gear." I took a sprinter's stance in the cramped space. "We'll grab a slice and a soda, scarf it down, and double time it to Kelli's."

Haley rolled her eyes, but I had her. She dashed off to the bathroom to finalize preparations for the evening's festivities. Standing back to full height, I was level with the benevolent shine in Gail's eyes.

"Nice job not taking the bait. I may owe you an apology. She's testing out some of the lines I made famous in the past. This one's on me."

"Thanks." I accepted the amends. "On the other hand, past skirmishes about timeliness have some basis in fact. I'm not sure what I'll do when she stops thinking I'm funny."

We reached the point in the conversation where I used to put my foot in my mouth with one of my verbal fishing expeditions, in hopes she still thought I was clever and wanted to go on a date. Times had changed. I got quiet. Before we had a chance to practice more mature adult communication, Haley flew back down the hall, her black Chuck Taylor high tops laced, her pink Lady Gaga bag fully loaded.

"Bye Mom." She fist-bumped Gail. "Let's roll, Dad!" She held up a ball of cash. "Did my chores. Pizza's on me." She bypassed the steps in a long jump from the porch.

"From mild hostility to I'm springing for dinner in five minutes or less. I guess we're good to go."

On the way to dinner, I listened to my daughter's tales of excitement—a new substitute teacher, breakups and reunions with friends, and the new kid from Afghanistan with a cool name and quiet manner.

"It's Amir."

I parked. "You like this fellow, huh."

She snorted and jumped from the Jeep. "Geez, Dad. Lighten up."

Busted.

"Or." She waited to hold the glass door open for me, scrunching her lips. "Maybe I should marry him."

I bowed to her superior wit.

Two ginormous slices of credible Des Moines pepperoni, green pepper, and onion satisfied the carnivore in both of us. Chewing allowed my mental revolving door time to skate between Haley's gibe, Seth Oberstreet's crisis, and other matters.

It ain't the best.

"Dad." Haley interrupted my thoughts, holding the remnants of an adequate crust. "Are you comparing this to Morningside Pizza again?"

The famed Morningside Pizza, consumed in mass quantities when I'd hitchhike from Ames to Sioux City to run the streets with my buddy, Tom, who attended the former Morningside College, now Morningside University.

"Caught me, kiddo. I heard the place has been passed down through the family. Best pizza ever."

"We could road trip it sometime," she deadpanned, a veteran of my passion for family food joints. "You know.

Eat pizza. Visit the site of the famous Sioux City stockyards. Hit the pool hall."

"Play table shuffle board." I grinned full on.

This kid has a future as the second funniest Anderson.

"Hey, Dad." Haley hit the bridge to our next topic at lightning speed. "Are you dating somebody?"

And the second most curious Anderson.

"Yes." Simple. True.

"Is it serious?"

"Not yet."

"Not yet," she mused. "Is it Jill?"

"Yes."

"When can the three of us get together?"

"Are you ready?"

"I think so. Are you ready?"

"I think so," I mirrored.

"Is she?"

"I don't know. I'll ask. How did you guess?"

"I saw how you looked at her when she dropped by last week." She did a Groucho Marx with her eyebrows. "Grandpa calls it googly eyes."

"Oh."

"Plus, the house has been really clean lately."

"Oh."

She patted me on the shoulder. "You want a soda refill?"

I slid my cup her way.

A Dr. Brown's crème soda refill and drive time discussion of the women's suffrage movement—the history project of choice—touched us down at Kelli's house, fashionably late.

"Kelli's parents are doing transport tonight. Great to see you, kiddo."

"You too, Dad." She opened the car door and paused. "You know I still get sad and mad that you and Mom aren't together."

"Understandable."

She fist-bumped me and launched from the Jeep.

"Thanks for dinner," I yelled as the door slammed shut.

With a thumbs up, she hurried off to change history. Kelli's mom let her in and gave me a peace sign.

On the drive back to Windsor Heights every available emotion—amazed, sad, happy, frustrated, excited, confused, guilty—cycled through me. They almost replaced my gnawing worry for another family's child.

THURSDAY

I woke with the blanket in knots, wound tight like the spring on the ageless alarm clock clanging—GET UP—in my ear. There had been no call from Phil the previous evening. I felt a tug of sympathy for farm families who most days rise in the dark to do morning chores, then shuffled downstairs to shower and dress for my outing in as little artificial light as my vision would allow.

When I moved to the garage, a ripple of gut butterfly turned up the volume on the day to come.

Not your typical ride in the country.

Yesterday, I required a bit of the Jeep's AC to cool down. This morning, a little heat. The paradox of fall in the Midwest. My thoughts skipped ahead to the cruel Iowa winter soon to require max heat and four-wheel drive.

I planned extra time to stop at a nearby all-night donut shop, large coffee with cream for me, large cup of black for Phil. Coffee and driving go together for me. Coffee and most things go together for me. I added the late, great Lyle Mays on CD, low volume; going for the correct blend of fluid jazz and caffeine wake-up.

Emotionally grounded and mentally alert. Science.

I cruised into the police department's central parking area fifteen minutes later. Phil was ready for me, headlights on. He had commandeered a black-on-white police sedan with one of those imposing battering rams on the front. I visualized the two of us slamming through a split-rail fence and going airborne to free Seth from the clutches of The Scholars of Calm.

Phil signaled from the car and pointed me toward visitor parking.

I slid into the passenger seat, reminded of several not-so-friendly rides during my misspent youth, courtesy of the hometown PD, most of whom regularly ate dinner at my parents' restaurant. The combination of solitary bookworm and unhappy kid run amok cost Mom a lot of sleep and plenty of extra broasted, not roasted, chicken for the folks in blue during my formative years.

"I like the view better from the front seat." I handed Phil his coffee.

"Thinking out loud again?"

"Sorry."

He let it go. "Ready?"

"Ready," I saluted. "So, Detective Evans, not in stealth mode. Lights and sirens?"

"Not today." His answer was free of discernible emotion. He took a sip of coffee. "And it's too early for you to try to be funny."

I let it go.

"You'll want to know." He came back to business, pulling into traffic. "I spoke with Seth's parents, who were both relieved that he'd been found and terrified that he is gone again. They reluctantly agreed to let us get a fix on his location before they book a flight for Des Moines. They will want to speak with us about his current condition as soon as possible."

"Let's hope we can bring them good news."

I stopped myself from the temptation to run grim scenarios on what his state of mind might be while we joined the other early risers, passing from still darkened strip malls to dimly lit housing developments to farmers and rural school bus drivers awake and at work.

Fifty-some minutes on a checkerboard of county roads took us in nervous silence to a gravel lane northeast of the city. At least I was nervous. Phil seemed his usual stoic self. Kicking up dust for a quarter mile, he eased the car onto the parched grass shoulder. We stepped from his rolling advertisement for law enforcement onto a pot-holed dirt entrance in front of a chain locked gate.

An old friend used to tell me that fear and excitement feel the same in your body. The bile in my throat confirmed his insight.

"Follow my lead," Phil instructed. "We're here to find the boy and make sure he's safe. Offer him a ride to somewhere other than here." He tapped a mechanism smaller than a thick cell phone attached to his XXL trench coat. Unfortunately, I'd seen them on the uniforms of officers at speed traps around the city.

Body cam.

"We'll also gather information," he said.

"What if they refuse to talk to us?"

"Won't happen."

"What if they ask us to leave?"

He squeezed his six-foot-five brickwork frame between the gate and a nasty mass of side brush. "Follow my lead," he repeated.

I swallowed the sense of physical inadequacy I often felt in the big man's company and forced myself through, my clothes collecting burrs he managed to escape. The gate stood guard over a path worn by tire tracks, dotted with ruts and anemic clumps of weeds. It was lined on both sides with unmowed meadow thick with enough dew to soak you to the knees. Mature oak trees wound through the woods to somewhere. The unusually gentle morning breeze carried intersecting scents of hay, cows, and fall wildflowers, an unrefined perfume appreciated by those who love the countryside.

People like me. I took a deep calming breath and waited for Phil to lead. He squared up his ever-present fedora and we set off down the trail he guaranteed would lead us to the camp.

The morning had slipped into daybreak, spears of light slicing through the gaps between trees. The suggestion of a moon still hovered above us. By noon I'd hope for a light pullover and jogging shorts. For now, my t-shirt, jeans, and corduroy sport coat were insufficient for Iowa's early morning contradiction—chill plus humidity.

A couple of football fields in length down the path, we rounded to the south and were met by an unnatural mixture of voices in song and the earthy smell of an open fire.

"Well, we know somebody's here," he said.

"Holy shit."

He gave me a pass on my profanity. "We're not trying to sneak up on them, so we can talk. Stay with me. Don't wander off. We'll be fine."

"Got it."

He shot me the side-eye. We had a checkered past involving his directives and my level of compliance.

Into a clearing, the makeshift road ended in the unkept yard of a derelict gray farmhouse large enough for several generations of family. The house was two stories, with shutters at least a decade beyond their original forest green, and a wraparound porch. On approach, the rest of the property took form. I scanned the hodgepodge of outbuildings: traditional faded red barn, free-standing garage with doors dangling from rusted hinges, and a crusty well pump. The lopsided remnants of a pre-indoor plumbing outhouse, on the edge of collapse, sat a safe distance from the house.

The landscape of my small-town Iowa childhood was scattered with much better and far worse renderings of this acreage.

I was most interested in a tin roofed pole barn. It harbored a large white cargo van and a road-weary pickup truck.

Red.

Ahead of us, a man stood at the bottom of sagging porch steps, monitoring our arrival. Curiosity buzzed through me.

Don't wander off.

The man clocked in somewhere in his late 20s, with blanched brown skin, flowing black hair and a lumberjack beard, flecked with premature gray. He wore a loose off-white shirt and formless off-white pants, forgoing any layers against the chill. He displayed one of those vacuous, blissful smiles common to people who approach you on the street with a handful of pamphlets to ask if you've found the path to true happiness right before they ask for money. His breath hit the crisp morning air in recycled puffs.

Beyond him in the uncut yard, huddled around a small bonfire, was a makeshift choir of young people in full voice.

My childhood in small-town Iowa was not full of renderings of whatever this represented.

"Good morning, Officer." The man noticed the body cam and formal dress, assuming Phil's origin without an introduction.

He's not a stranger to contact with police.

"Detective Evans," Phil corrected. Opening his coat, he flashed the gold shield hanging from his belt. "Good morning, Lawrence."

We know who you are, too, creep.

"How can I help you?" The faux Maharishi tone of his voice announced he was not the least bit interested in being helpful.

Phil went for casual with a head nod toward the collection of young people on our left. "Getting the day started?"

"Inspirational song and breakfast." Lawrence swept his hand past the choir to a rickety card table with bowls, a gallon jug of milk, and the plastic bags of cereal I remembered well from one of the budget crunches common to our family during Dad's drinking years. It tasted like sugared Styrofoam.

I detached from the conversation to scan the faces of the young women and men, directed by another white-clad male. The choir was uniformly dressed in the same peasant get-up Seth had worn to my office. As a whole, they were not familiar with time signature or singing in key.

No Seth.

I strained to make out the words they repeated ad nauseum:

Peace among us
Serve the greater good
Love among us
Serve the greater good
We are The Scholars of Calm
Calm among us
Calm among us
Calm among us
Calm among us
We are The Scholars of Calm
Serve the greater good

Phil was a serious Methodist and I had milled around a lot of churches as a kid in the Christian bread basket. This song didn't ring any bells. It was a chant. Led by a person cloned from The Scholars of Calm handbook.

The resonance of Phil's greeting reached the maestro, who turned and dropped his arms. The choir sputtered to a fractured end, aware that a large, uninvited black man and his compact white sidekick had shown up.

"We're here to visit with Seth Oberstreet."

"He's not here, Detective." Lawrence emphasized Phil's title, exposing an impatience that ran counter to his saintly veneer. "We took Brother Seth to the bus station last evening, immediately after he visited with Mr. Anderson." Lawrence's counterfeit serenity mutated into a staged look of concern. "He seemed more, not less, upset after they met."

Contempt. And a liar.

"We determined he needed to return home."

"Where exactly is home?" Phil prodded, even though he had the answer.

"We would have to gather that information and contact you."

"There's no we." The anger leaked through my resolve to let Phil direct the action. "You brought him to my office and then you took him to the bus station. Where did you send him?"

Phil gave my outburst time to register, then took another step toward the man. "So, you claim someone, whoever picked Seth up from Mr. Anderson's office, put this vulnerable young man on a bus by himself, without his belongings, and sent him to a location you can't recall without consulting your records."

Lawrence's benevolent facade showed a crack.

Phil didn't wait for a reply. "We'll look around to make sure."

"That won't be possible, unless you have a warrant."

"Something to hide?" It was more of an accusation than a question.

"I am charged with the maintenance of our sacred environment." He opened his arms in a grand gesture, as if a malnutritioned property full of undernourished kids was a tabernacle just this side of paradise.

"I don't require your permission or a warrant, Lawrence." Phil was matter-of-fact. "Mr. Anderson and I are here to do a wellness check."

Calm and forceful was Phil at his best. He motioned me to hold steady and walked toward the false guru. Lawrence, as if compelled by the power of my friend's intent, backpedaled until his calves touched the stairs. Phil stayed close, inches from physical contact, and climbed to the porch. When he knocked on the washed-out front door, slivers of aged varnish fluttered in the breeze. He turned the tarnished knob and pushed it open, his non-threatening bass putting the choir to shame.

"Seth. Seth Oberstreet. Hank Anderson and Detective Phil Evans here to check in with you."

We waited.

No one answered. No one came.

I had a brush with nausea when Phil didn't enter the house. Instead, he left the door ajar, stepped back, and retraced his steps to the lawn. I stutter stepped forward, but his eyes held me in place. He steered to his left and, with painstaking care, examined each outbuilding. He orbited the pole barn, approached the rear end of the truck, circled to the front, looked through the windshield, and opened the driver's side. I watched the eyes of the entire ramshackle congregation follow his every move.

Apparently satisfied, the detective ambled back and stopped a safe distance from the group of timid singers, still as statues, their clouds of breath meeting chill the only signs of life.

"Good morning. My name is Detective Phil Evans of the Des Moines Police Department. This is my colleague, Mr. Anderson. We are here to make sure Seth Oberstreet is safe and, if what we have been told is true, on his way home. Can any of you confirm that Seth is no longer on this property?" All eyes, save one set, shifted to Lawrence or dropped, staring vacantly into the grass. A striking young woman with auburn hair past her shoulders gave Phil what Dad calls, "the once over." But no one spoke.

"You are not in trouble," Phil said. "We are here to help your friend."

Nothing.

I edged a couple of paces toward the group.

Maybe I'm less threatening.

"We'd like to help you, too. If anyone wants to leave with Detective Evans and myself, we have plenty of room."

Another reinterpretation of following Phil's lead.

"Yes." He backed me up. "We have plenty of room."

The silence was profound, the only sound coming from the racket of a fleet of barn swallows inserting themselves into the tension. These folks were either happy with their circumstance, or, like Seth, embroiled in the deprivation and indoctrination process. The circle of blank faces made it easy to guess which it was.

Phil reached into his pocket and moved to the breakfast table. He placed several of his cards next to the bowls. I did the same. His lip twitched, but he patted each stack.

"Feel free to contact either of us if you have any information or concerns." He centered in on Lawrence. "I'll be in contact with you again. Soon." I wanted to believe I saw Lawrence flinch at the threat. Phil turned to me. "Let's go." He backed up, rotated, and returned the way we came.

Unable to immediately grasp the idea that we were leaving empty-handed, I stood flat-footed, feeling the energy of Lawrence's hatred fill the space between us. I held his glare with my own and conveyed what I hoped was a look of deep concern to the group before backpedaling and trailing Phil up the path, prepared to apologize for leapfrogging over his instructions. With effort, I sat on my words.

"I'm sorry. I messed up." We were back on the two-lane, heading into the city when he finally restarted the conversation.

"You're sorry? I'm the one who jumped in and offered your squad car as a taxi service."

"A good idea," he said. "I wish we'd gotten more takers than we could fit in the squad car; I'd have called for more help. The fact that no one took you up on the offer tells us how much control this man has over those kids. I believed Seth would be at the camp and we would bring him out of there, putting Lawrence on the back foot. I underestimated him."

"Why didn't we go in the house?"

"These are kids to you and me, but, in truth, they are college age adults. They did not look to be in immediate physical danger, nor did anyone say they were being held against their wishes. No obvious crime is being committed. By Lawrence's statement and the non-responsive group, Seth is no longer there. He was half right. I had no warrant to go further than a wellness check on an individual who Lawrence claims is headed for home. I had the Sheriff Department's clearance to go into the county to follow up on a matter that started in the city, but I didn't ask them for back up. I was tempted to cross the line, but couldn't."

I'm the line crosser.

"Next question. Is Lawrence really Taranis?"

"I'm not sure. Yet. One of our people is researching this organization. Tyr Taranis is the supposed Enlightened One. He's elusive. No photos in their materials." He pointed at the camera on his chest. "Now we have pictures."

"By the way, Tyr was the Norwegian god of justice and Taranis was the Celtic Thunder god."

"Is that a fact." Sometimes I surprised Phil.

"I read a lot of mythology as a kid."

"Well, it fits. What we have so far tells us Taranis has declared himself at the center of a new movement," he continued. "Until now, they've run a few start-up groups close to college campuses. This is different. These kids were transported hundreds of miles from home to a farmhouse in Iowa. Based on the deprivation you observed with Seth, and what we witnessed this morning, the department will be taking a much closer look at this cult."

I choked on the remains of my lukewarm coffee.

Cult.

"We'll know by the end of the day who owns the farm and how they got in," he said, slowing for the suburbs. "One more thing."

My brain was still on the word I'd left unspoken.

"The red truck. Same one?"

I nodded, catching my breath.

"It had an up-to-date Wyoming plate. No letters WK. Not green and white."

I locked back in. "They changed plates."

"They changed plates." He tapped his body cam. "But they couldn't change the VIN number."

I was only slightly reassured to know that the detective's walkabout had been more than theater for the benefit of his audience.

Phil lapsed back into quiet. He's one of the few people in my life for whom long periods without speaking seems normal. He was thinking. I was thinking. Riding through the morning rush hour we kept those thoughts to ourselves. By the time he dropped me at my Jeep, he was ready for another round.

"I'll determine whether Seth got on the bus to Denver. I'll put somebody on identifying the other kids. We'll identify Lawrence and track down who holds the registrations on their vehicles." His expression went flat. "I'll also notify Seth's parents of our failure to find him onsite."

Horrible part of his job.

"One more thing," he said. "Did you notice the young woman who didn't look away? Maybe she had something to tell us, but couldn't speak in front of the others."

"Seth mentioned a friend. Emma. Could be her."

"Now she knows the police are involved. Perhaps we'll hear from her."

I had my own questions. "You saw how Lawrence reacted to me. Why bring Seth to a therapist? Exposing themselves to the outside world should have been the last thing on these peoples' agenda."

"Theories?"

"Seth's nightmares scared them."

And something I can't quite grab on to.

"Which doesn't explain, why not simply send him away?"

"We'll know when we pin them down." Bravado was a weak replacement for a plausible answer. "One last thing from my end. Lawrence lied. Seth told me he felt better after we met, not worse. At the end of the session, we had a nanosecond of standing together on solid ground."

"Something changed when he got in the truck."

"Lawrence heard something he didn't like. Or, Seth regressed further when they got back to the camp."

"Another question I will get answered."

I will get answered. Something's off here.

I unlatched the door, wrestling with a new concern. "This in another tough one, huh."

"There is more to be done. Thanks for backing me up."

Deflection.

"Belinda gave me permission to attend the outing, as long as I had appropriate supervision."

"She is acutely aware of your proclivity for risk and trouble."

I thumped him on the shoulder.

"Pal, you are the master of polite understatement."

Phil sat alone in the squad car after Hank pulled out of the parking lot. Every ounce of his friend's worries piled onto his own. The weight attached itself to an abiding pain the strongman knew could drive him to his knees. He hid it well, but Hank was one of the most intuitive people he had ever known. More questions were soon to come. Questions beyond The Scholars of Calm.

A casual salute from an overnight road officer heading home shook him from his trance. He loosened his grip on the steering wheel. He needed backup. His partner picked up immediately.

"Good morning, Dale. No, it didn't go well." He scanned the gated officers' lot and spotted Goodman's personal sedan. "Can you meet me out front?" He listened. "Yes, now. The coffee's on me."

He hung up and rifled through his contacts for a personal number. His next call went to voicemail.

"You've reached Michael Jordan, the Polk County Deputy, not the basketball legend. Leave your message."

"Deputy. Phil Evans. We visited The Scholars of Calm camp this morning. There were people present, but the young man we're concerned about was not among them. I'm on my way to obtain a warrant to search the property. I'm hoping you're available. I'd appreciate a call."

He watched Dale shuffle out the front door of the building, suit coat open, his tie already at half-mast.

A return text popped up.
I'm in. Will call for details after my meeting.

Phil allowed himself a glimmer of relief as Goodman wedged his body into the car, eyeballing the back seat.

"Looks like you didn't find the kid," he said. "And we're going out of the house for coffee."

Phil was reminded of the many people, including Hank, who sold Dale short based on his unrefined exterior and coarse manner.

"Now you need my help." Dale sounded hurt.

"I decided it was too early in the day to hear you and Hank banter." The two shared a caustic style of interaction that could hit the limits of Phil's considerable tolerance.

"I wrapped up our paperwork on the robbery in the East Village. One of the clerks, caught on camera after hours, carrying boxes of t-shirts out the back door with a buddy. Who says criminals are stupid? Oh. I did." Phil knew the victory lap was Dale's code for—let's move on. "I believe this bust is worth a large coffee, partner."

"We can do a drive-through on the way to the courthouse."

"Courthouse." Goodman ran a hand over his perpetually world-weary expression. "If you make it a stop at Donut King, I'll let you give me the check list on the new case you have in your head. The one that's going to keep us busy and complicate my life."

Dale knew him pretty well, too.

~~~

On the drive home, I attempted to free the miserable outcome of our sunrise surprise from my head with maximum decibels of a guilty pleasure, a seventies country rock compilation. Pondering Michael Nesmith's trek from make believe rock star on The Monkees TV show to his seminal country tune, *Different Drum,* Linda Ronstadt's first hit, almost replaced the commotion in my head.

The welcome sight of my bicycle in the garage offered additional diversion from a general sense of helplessness. I made a quick call to the office of my former attorney, Jill Bennett, traded my business uniform for silly looking biking shorts, ran a quick check of air pressure, brakes and spin, and wheeled out of the garage before Belinda's intuition told her to track me down and assign me something else to do. As expected, the fall nip had burned off and given rise to a mild Field of Dreams kind of day, full of color and surprisingly free of the headwinds that were part and parcel of most Iowa warming trends.

I didn't have time for a serious ride to the magnificent High Trestle Trail, the decommissioned railroad line paved across the thirteen-story high bridge over the Des Moines River. I made a mental note to invite

Dennis and his husband, Jerry, for a ride. After Phil and I found Seth.

Today, I weaved my way through the side streets and caught the Clive Greenbelt Trail, reminding myself that a solitary ride can be as seductive and hazardous as smooth-talking spiritualists. The constant hum of narrow tires on asphalt, the rhythmic click of shifting gears, and the repetition of circular motion is hypnotic. Lulled into inattention, a rider can abruptly greet pavement, wiping out on a patch of stray rock or a crack in the roadway. I cringed at memories of how little protection is provided when spandex hits gravel or concrete. My concentration on the road ahead provided a temporary freedom from the ominous word Phil used to label The Scholars of Calm. I breathed in the aroma of summer surrendering to fall, hoping Seth had spent the night breathing in the odors of stale bus air and fast food on his journey home.

An hour later, I coasted off the bike path, back onto the street, tuned into the heavy traffic and a shoulder filled with debris. Rolling through an intersection, I locked eyes with the driver of an oncoming delivery van.

"CAR!" She screamed out her open window, frantically gesturing behind me.

From muscle memory, I broke into a rushing sweat and veered to the right. My front tire exploded in the crunch of chipped glass and twigs. Something metal and unforgiving thumped the meat of my upper arm, pushing me to a dead-stop at the curb. I launched forward, man separated from machine, ass over teakettle. I had a split second to avoid extending my arms, the ultimate biking error; hands first falls result in broken collar-bones. Instead, momentum hurled me onto dry, yellowed grass, shoulder then helmet, my nose filling with dust. I bounced, a jumbled pile of limbs skidding to a stop short of the sidewalk.

"Damn!" I held still for whatever scorching pain would follow the adrenaline rush. A sneeze cleared my nose.

"Damn!" My head rebelled, but no key limbs screamed at me and no blood gushed from my body.

Convinced that all of my parts were still connected, I uncurled and worked my way to my feet. Weak in the knees, I shivered as if the temperature had dropped to single digits, leaning against a convenient maple tree, my breath coming in blasts.

Slow. You're alive. Breathe. Slow.

While my heartbeat regulated, I rested my head against the trunk and surveyed the street. Traffic moved on, unaware that a potentially fatal crash had happened.

But, my body told me it most certainly had. I felt a lump begin to stretch the skin on my arm, throbbing in 4/4 time. I felt, before I saw, my raw, dusty knees. I unbuckled and eased the helmet from my head. A hairline fracture showed through to the foam padding. The possibility that an ugly hat of beveled plastic had saved my assaulted brain pan from permanent damage took me back to the ground, my back against the tree.

"You okay?"

A heavily bearded man in a washed-out flannel shirt cut above his substantial biceps stood over me. A transit van with Paul's Premeer Plumbing in glossy blue letters on the side had pulled onto the grass up the block.

"A whole lot better than I might have been."

"You need an ambulance? Or a ride to the hospital?" He pointed his thumb at the van.

"I don't think so."

He pointed at my bike. "Well, you definitely need a ride home."

"Aw, man!" I yelled, flinching at the beginnings of a monster headache. My disabled machine lay on its battered side. The rim on my front wheel was beyond bent, my tire sliced flat. Spokes stuck out every which way. My front brakes were toast.

"How about I load the bike and give you a lift." The Good Samaritan extended a hand. "I'm Paul." Favoring my arm, I let him help me to my feet.

"I'm Hank."

I stood, held up by the tree, while Paul loaded the bike in the back of a well-organized travelling office, shelves filled with mysterious pipes and tools of his trade, the floor spotless, a hinged work table latched against the side panel. I steadied myself and shuffled my scraped body and awkward clip-in cycling shoes into the passenger seat.

My new friend was a talker. Turned out his last name was Premeer. Pronounced like it was spelled. He specialized in commercial work, resigned to jobs in the uninspired glass and chrome office buildings springing up as Des Moines sprawled ever westward. His monologue engaged me until I was deposited on my front lawn, alongside my sad bicycle.

"Paul, did you happen to see whatever sideswiped me?"

"Sure did. Black SUV. The driver smacked you pretty hard with the side mirror. It had those tinted windows. Happened so fast I didn't get a license number, but it wasn't an Iowa plate. They probably didn't see you."

"I guess not. Anyway, thanks. You're a good man."

"Just doing the right thing." He deflected in customary Midwestern form. "Good luck and take it slow."

I watched him head off to his next job.

Lots of good people in Des Moines. Not counting the ones who do hit-and-run.

I fished the door opener from the twisted frame of my seat bag and dragged the bike into the garage.

I'm going to have some serious bruises. And a hell of a story for the repair folks at the shop.

My arm told me not to lift the damaged machine onto the ceiling hook. I propped it against the wall, depositing the life-saving helmet on a shelf where it would forever shout—Never Leave Home Without Your Helmet. I hobbled through the side door, peeling my shredded biking kit on the way to the shower. While the water beat my muscles, I ran the wreck through my impaired problem-solving filter to fend off reflexive anxiety.

Didn't see me. It happens. Distracted driver. Easy to miss one guy on a bike. No black SUV at the farm. No way they didn't feel the impact. Why didn't the driver stop?

I shuddered through a sequence of flashbacks of home invasions perpetrated by the dangerous men caught in Kenny Jensen's game of misdirection. Three lives were ended. I got to live.

Did somebody tried to kill me? Again?

My legs rubberized and I sank to the shower floor. Waiting to run out of hot water, one simple lesson from those terrible nights pushed through my cumulative trauma response.

Call Phil.

I forced myself up and out. Drenched and dripping on the guest room carpet, I ran another body check. Free of grass stains and dirt, my knees, elbows, and hip were enflamed, scratched bright red with road rash. Some unknown muscle in my upper arm was already sporting an ugly bruise.

The good news. No nausea. No dizziness. No double vision. No neck pain.

No concussion. You're not a doctor, Anderson, but you are experienced at falling on your head.

The best news. Not dead.

I downed several horse pill sized ibuprofen and made a careful climb up the first landing to my fortress of solitude, an attic turned bedroom by the previous owner. I dressed in a long sleeve Santana t-shirt and loose jogging pants guaranteed not to constantly remind me of my tender bits and pieces, and went looking for my oft-misplaced phone. If I'd put shoes on, I would have jumped out of them when the doorbell rang. Going into stealth mode, I checked the peephole in the front door, another habit born of my recent past.

Jill.

Form hugging cream colored business suit. Emerald green silk blouse. The late-day sun painted a golden aura around her porcelain, lightly freckled skin and strawberry hair. She carried a black leather briefcase.

Wow.

Jill Bennett and I had wandered in and out of one another's orbit after she concluded her efforts as my attorney on the heels of Jake the thug's death. She ran interference for me legally, becoming a friend when I struggled to accept the outcome of the first mess in the fall. A dinner here. A bicycle ride there. A couple of near misses on my sofa on hard-boiled mystery movie nights.

I'd been honest, letting Jill know my body temperature hit the red zone when I thought about her. Her imagery had been less intense, but no less colorful.

"I'm guessing you're the Little Engine That Could, Anderson." She referred to my previously documented combination of modest height and king-size get-up-and-go. "That makes me nervous."

She poked the bell a few more times.

Open the door, Anderson.

"Can I help you with something, Counselor?"

"Probably not. But, let me in anyway, Anderson."

It's cool when she uses the third person.

"Please come in."

She squeezed my shoulder.

"Ouch."

"What?" She stopped and rested her fingertips on my chaffed face.

"Bumped my chin today."

Her eyes bore into my omission.

"My chin and arm. Fell off the bike. I'll tell you about it over dinner."

"Yes, you will." She answered in her official—Judge, the witness is being uncooperative—voice, then switched gears.

"Hope I didn't cross a line by coming early."

"Well, I have to clear the blonde out of my bedroom. But take a seat on the sofa and I'll sneak her out the side door."

Lame.

She opened her briefcase and fetched a long blue-on-gray Drake Bulldogs Law School sweatshirt, and what was bound to be a pair of seriously snug yoga pants, from its depths. "Take your time. I'll pop into the bathroom and slip into these."

"Early is great. You change. I'll cook."

I'd gone big-time with the menu: BBQ shrimp pasta, a recipe I pieced together from conversations with Steven, the reticent chef at my favorite neighborhood Italian bistro. Adding fresh garlic bread and a salad of greens, tomatoes, cucumbers, slices of red cabbage, and my famous homemade creamy Italian dressing, engaged my hope to revise a timeworn platitude—the way to a woman's heart is through her stomach.

I cued up the newly released album by my buddy and alarm system tech, James, whose band, Slippery When Wet, was beginning to break out beyond the Des Moines club scene. The melodic ska of the opening track boomed through serious Klipsch surround sound, an original tune with lyrics that included the Iowa Cubs Triple-A baseball team, right-wing politics, systemic racism, the state fair, and the heartache caused by a woman on a Harley named Rebecca.

Soundtrack for food prep in place, I commenced to slice and dice, allowing thoughts of Seth and a brush with death to nibble at the edges, my aching brain attempting to connect the series of disjointed events. The only progress I made was tidy mounds of white onion, red pepper, and fresh garlic.

Fighting to find links in a chain of ideas is like writer's block, Hank. The size of the blank page is equal to the degree of strain.

Embracing the wisdom of my former, and probably future, therapist, Bob Rathburn, I pivoted and stripped the cobs of the last ears of the season's best local sweetcorn for texture, letting myself wander to reminiscences of an eighteen-year internship in the southwest Iowa eatery owned by my parents, J.R. and Sheila Anderson. We were the real deal: homemade potato salad and coleslaw, hand-breaded onion rings, the best Coney Dog sauce west of Detroit, and the secret Anderson recipe for broasted chicken. I became a decent cook. Dennis says I have a secondary gig if the psychotherapy thing doesn't work out.

Mom died more than five years back. Too many cigarettes and too little self-care. For the most part, she took care of others. Dad still runs the operation, his love for his wife enmeshed with the pain we all experienced during his years of active alcoholism. In sobriety, he'd become one of the wisest people I knew.

Jill disrupted my musings in the best way, making her appearance in the kitchen with a shimmering grace. I took the stereo volume down a notch as James and the band moved into a rocking cover of the Bill Wither's classic, *Lovely Day*. She sat and watched while I added shrimp and adorned the sauce with Hank's secret spices.

"I was already at the courthouse when you called the office, but Justin decided I needed to be free tonight," she said.

I'd reached Justin, Jill's paralegal, before my second dodgy outing of the morning, thinking dinner company would be a nice compliment to a leisurely bike ride. When the day went further sideways, I missed his second message. Her case had settled. He determined I would be no less than thrilled if she showed up early.

I liked Justin.

"I'll set the table." She rummaged through the cupboards and drawers and voila, the countertop where Haley and I ate most of our meals was ready to go.

I went with string phenom Rhiannon Giddens for dinner music, sparkling water on the side. I learned early in my relationship with Jill that she was a friend of Bill W's, code for Bill Wilson, one of the founders of Alcoholics Anonymous. We met through Dennis, who had introduced her to AA and sobriety, what devotees call the Program. I carry a profound respect for those who walk the walk of addiction recovery. Dad. Dennis. Jill. People who found sobriety, then went about the business of sharing their experience, strength and hope with other seekers.

As for myself. I do Al-Anon, the self-help group for those folks who love those folks.

"Great people."

"Thinking out loud, Anderson?"

I pointed my fork at her. "Just a moment of reflection on the delightful people I've met through the Program."

"Like me."

"Like you."

"Good food. Rhiannon Giddens for tunes. Fellow Program nerd in the kitchen." She pointed her fork back at me. "Excellent."

Allowing plenty of space, we kept jobs and bodily injuries off the table, each going seconds on carbs.

"I like a woman who knows her way around a plate of pasta."

"Do people really think you're funny?"

"No, but funny people are like other artists, often misunderstood."

She tossed her napkin at me.

She likes me.

"How about I do clean-up."

"No way, Counselor. This is a full-service establishment."

"I'll put on more music."

I like to go old school on kitchen duty. Standing at the sink over an assortment of pans, my body did the red zone thing when she cued up the next album.
Marvin Gaye.
I heard her bare feet glide across the floor. Her forehead rested on my good shoulder. I turned into her.
"You like Marvin?"
"Love Marvin."
"Maybe the second shift can finish the dishes."
With few words and considerable noise, dusk dancing through the patio doors found us tangled and spent on the sofa. I managed to pretend my body didn't hurt until I forgot it hurt. Nothing athletic; just the urgency of two people who'd been out of circulation for a while.
I pulled a fleece throw over us to capture the heat we'd generated.
"You're an amazing woman."
"Yes, I am."

~~~

Another insufferable day with these whiny fools. He wanted to punch somebody.
"Lawrence, I'm tired."
"Embrace the chi of the universe, Sister."
"Thank you, Lawrence."
"I'm hungry, Lawrence."
"Embrace the sustenance of the cosmos, Brother."
"I will, Lawrence."

His inner sneer almost wiped away the false benevolence he wore as a mask. He didn't say, give life on the streets a try, you pampered wimps. He certainly didn't tell them that wearing the group down was the whole idea. Up early. Bad food. Sing. Meditate. Weed the garden. Bad food. Sing. Meditate. Go to bed. Repeat.

A knife-like jab tried to cut through his belly, amplifying his secret tirade. On top of the energy it took to corral the kids, he was sick. Stomach pain. Sore throat. Nausea. His nose felt like it was stuffed with cotton balls.

Probably all the damn country air. Fresh. Not hardly. Manure. Burning wood. Whatever the hell they were cutting down in those fields. He longed for the smell of burgers and pizza floating out the open door of a greasy spoon. The sweaty odor of steam rising off the streets after a storm on a scorching hot day. A shot backed up by a beer. City life.

The whole job had been gummed up with complications brought on by that bobble head, Seth, triggering a visit from your friendly neighborhood cop and that bleeding-heart Anderson. He'd maintained the pretense of cooperation, making sure to plant the seed that Seth needed to go home after meeting with the shrink.

Still. The message on the burner phone had ripped into him.

"You made a colossal mistake. Fix it. Get control. Get the information. Deal with the kid."

The pain in his stomach doubled him over. It was true. He had panicked. Moved too far from the plan. By the time they knew the info coughed up by the kid was bogus, the guy was pretty far down the hill to crazy town.

But, he could fix this. Seth still trusted him. Give him a little rest. A good meal. Dial down the dietary supplements. Finish the job. After a little attitude adjustment of his own.

Hearing no movement in the house, he locked the door on the only private room, his, and went to the closet for a special devotional.

What was his pleasure? Maybe crush up a bit of first-class something or other from the bag he designated for stress management. Enough to take the edge off a tough day, clear his sinuses, help him plot their next move.

He opened the first of the cardboard boxes hidden in the back. His stomach clenched. Gone! Scrambling on his hands and knees, he ripped open the second box and dug, clutching the pile of baggies buried under a stack of androgynous white clothes.

"Get a grip, man," he mumbled.

Standing too quickly, he stumbled, dizzy and short of breath. He steadied himself against the door frame before sinking onto the bed with his stash.

Nothing a little bump and a nap couldn't mend.

Tonight. Close things out. Tomorrow. Vanish. All expenses paid.

Dave Brubeck's *Take Five* intruded on our comfort.

"Don't answer it," Jill said.

Six rings and Dave's quartet ran out of notes in 5/4 time. Somebody immediately hit redial. Goosebumps rippled up my arms.

"Not a coincidence." She unraveled from me and drifted in the direction of the music. "Hello. Yes, Detective. Jill Bennett. He's right here. Let me put him on."

I forgot to call Phil.

She stood on the steps into the sunken living room, one hand on her hip, phone in the other. I wrapped myself in the blanket, collected the cursed object, and unmuted. Remembering her house tour from our second date, Jill turned and swayed in her ample glory toward the stairs to my cocoon-like bedroom. I watched her curves disappear into the darkness.

Wow.

"Hank?" His voice sounded like an overworked diesel engine.

"I'm here Phil?"

"Sorry to call late."

Nothing about Jill. Ever the gentleman.

"You wouldn't have called twice unless it was important." My prefrontal cortex kicked back in. "Did you find Seth?"

"Dale and I went back to the camp with Deputy Jordan from the Sheriff's Department this evening, with a warrant."

"And."

"The truck and van were gone. The camp was empty. Of almost everybody."

"Almost?" My chest tightened.

"Except Lawrence. He's dead."

Not Seth.

"Dead? An accident?"

"We're investigating."

That means no.

"What about Seth?"

"Someone with his ID bought a ticket for the 6:15 bus to Denver last night, which would have put him in downtown Denver sometime this morning. His parents haven't heard from him and he's not answering his phone. We're following up at the Des Moines and Denver bus stations."

"Where did the rest of them go?"

"If I knew I'd tell you. We're investigating."

"Yeah. Sorry."

"We do know how they were able to use the property. Family farmhouse, well off the beaten path, left vacant when a widow, Mrs. Karlsson, died six years ago. Most of the acreage had been sold off years before she passed. No surviving family members. Somehow, Taranis knew it was abandoned. They went survivalist. Propane. Candles. Creek water for cold storage."

"They didn't plan to hunker down for an Iowa winter."

"No. When I get more, I'll let you know. I'm sorry to intrude on your evening."

"Sorry to do the same to you."

"What else have you got?"

I gave him the details of today's collision, including my thinker's block.

And there it is.

"Got it," I said.

"What?"

"Something Paul told me that didn't register at the time. He couldn't read the plate on the SUV, but it wasn't from Iowa."

"What colors?"

"He didn't say."

"I'm adding a black SUV to our team's follow up," he said. "We'll contact Mr. Premeer."

"Lawrence found another vehicle, drove it to town, located me on my bike, tried to kill me, then drove back to the farm to die? That's a lot of moving parts."

"I don't like coincidences. I'm glad you weren't seriously hurt." I'd learned he changed the subject when he wasn't interested in my opinion.

"Thanks."

"Another question. Did Seth say anything more about this fellow, Levi?"

"Only that he broke one of Lawrence's rules and got thrown out. Why?"

"We're beginning to identify the missing students and notify families. He doesn't show up anywhere. No police reports from family. He's gone."

"Gone the way of Lawrence?" I winced at the casual sound of my question.

"We're continuing to investigate."

Another non-answer.

"Do you have the high-tech security system James installed turned on, Hank?"

"Yes." The line got quiet. "I'll make sure."

"Good. I don't need to ask why you didn't call me sooner."

Phil was a class guy, but he was annoyed. Offering an account of recent events with Jill as my excuse seemed like a bad direction to go on every level.

"My apologies. Goodnight."

My legs were leaden. It had been that kind of day.

Remembering I had a special guest, I double-checked the locks, confirmed the security alarm and motion sensors were on ready, and stood rigid in the dark.

The strain in his voice. There's something more. Talk to Jill. Tell her what happened.

I retreated to the bedroom. My internal GPS knew the way. I stopped at the threshold, taking in the outline of her body. She'd made an honest effort to stay awake. Curled under the comforter, the nightlight on, my bedside copy of a dog-eared Walter Mosley novel rested in her hand. She released her grip without waking. I placed it on the night table, adding my favorite Iowa State University stadium blanket for extra warmth before slipping into bed. I closed my eyes, memorizing the sight, the smell, the feel of her, enlivened by the first woman in my bed since the divorce. My mind drifted through the night's events. I rarely had difficulty shutting down but tonight was special on levels both wonderful and deeply disturbing.

I'll call Phil again tomorrow. A wellness check.

Not much of a plan, but I slept.

~~~

Phil lay motionless, trying not to wake his wife. It wasn't Lawrence's face fixed in the agony of a horrendous death that made sleep impossible. It had most assuredly been brutal. On his back, hands gripping his stomach, bubbles of dried blood mixed with saliva stuck to his beard, ending in a puddle on the shabby down comforter. Bags of pills scattered across the floor. A mortar and pestle with the residue of yet to be determined substances resting on a battered walnut night stand scattered with white powder.

Sadly, Phil had seen worse.

He found some solace in the belief that a formerly dangerous man would now have to make his peace with forces beyond anyone's control or understanding.

It was the kids who haunted him. Seth and his friends. It was the families. Fearful of a loss unlike any other. A loss he understood.

Then there was Hank. He felt a deep-seated need to protect his friend.

Catherine rolled to his side, laying her arm across his barrel chest.

"You have done everything you can do for one day, Phillip." This was not the first time she'd whispered those words in his ear over the years. "You will do more tomorrow and you'll do it better with rest. Now, go to sleep."

He laid his hand over hers and pretended he could.

Tomorrow, he would find the students.

FRIDAY

Dad says he had days after a binge when, "I needed toothpicks to keep my eyes open." Drawn awake by a dream already lost to me, I could have used a hydraulic lift just to get started. I went for the right eye first. I was alone in bed. The sun sneaking into the room's single skylight told me it was morning. Going for broke, I opened the left.

I hurt all over.

Bike wreck, Anderson. And sex.

Empty. A tidy handwritten note lay where Jill had slept. I read it with a minimum of movement.

Had a great night. Sorry I couldn't stay awake. Thanks for the extra blanket. Left for an early meeting. I heard you moan In your sleep. You still owe me an explanation. Hope to see you soon.

Playful. Edgy. Unexpected progress in the continuing mystery of my romantic life.

Early meeting. It's Friday.

I was also due at the office sooner than later.

Lawrence.

˙   My primary feeling about the man had been disgust, but I didn't wish him dead.

Slowing my thoughts to match my pain, I sat up and maneuvered my feet to the floor. Testing for retrograde damage, not surprised to find the bruise on my arm taking on the colors of the rainbow, I stood—tender, stiff, but ambulatory. On the way to the shower, I went another round of extra strength ibuprofen and checked my phone.

No messages from Phil. No Seth.

I risked a few light stretches and dressed carefully. Remembering the previous morning's walk in the woods, a lightweight sweater seemed like a good addition to my traditional gear of buttoned-down shirt and jeans. Pocketing Jill's note, in case I needed a pick-me-up later in the day, I made my way through the kitchen. She had finished the dishes, made coffee the color of washed-out clay, and left Haley's box of Cheerios on the counter.

Industrious, but not raised by cooks.

Avoiding her coffee, I elected to take a detour to my favorite caffeine and donut haunt in route to the office. I looked both ways to rule out the possibility of killer vehicles before pulling into the street. The school bus on the corner seemed innocent enough. I waited for the kids to board, exchanged greetings with the driver and motored on, energized by the prospect of a quality cup of joe.

I need to research colloquialisms for coffee.

Ahmed, the most polite shop owner in the metro area, added a black coffee and two extra apple fritters to my usual order, with no mention of my battered chin.

"Thank you very much and thank you for your business, Mr. Anderson." I'd long ago given up my quest to get him to address me by my first name.

"Thank you for having the best coffee in town, Ahmed. Don't ever retire and remember, I will pay any price for your wife's apple fritters."

"I thank you and my wife thanks you. I will make sure to tell her again. Have a good day." He smiled his appreciation for my pastry worship.

Tempted to eat a bag full of fritters in the scant time needed to make it to our building, I showed an amazing amount of resolve.

"Morning, Belinda."

"Good morning." Belinda was behind her computer, busy at what she does best four days a week. Organizing our lives.

"Morning, Marlowe." My partner added his usual greeting. Some years back, Dennis, the Greenberg of Anderson & Greenberg Counseling, nicknamed me Marlowe, Jr. This was a play on Phillip Marlowe, novelist supreme Raymond Chandler's legendary gumshoe and a poke at my attraction to sticking my nose into dark and dangerous corners of the world. What began as sarcasm had become a pseudonym of endearment. It fits.

He was back in the office from a seminar on addiction and public health in Chicago, his husband Jerry's hometown. Dennis was his usual dapper self in a transitional fall wardrobe of tan cashmere jacket, open necked starched white dress shirt, and chocolate brown razor creased, "they're trousers, not pants," wandering our modest suite with the sullen expression of a man who hadn't saved time for his own caffeine stop. I picked up on his fear of drinking a cup of what Belinda had spent a decade passing off as coffee.

"It's water. It's ground coffee beans," he groused. "How can it be so awful?"

"I heard you Dennis. It's fine. I drink it."

"You're braver than I, Belinda."

I raised my to-go tray of the breakfast of champions to eye level and his face lit up like a kid who'd just won Best Turkey Call at the Iowa State Fair, replaced in a blink with suspicion.

"Fritters and black coffee. What's this going to cost me?" Deductive reasoning and experience.

"I was desperate. Belinda and Jill must have gone to the same barista school."

Oops.

"Jill?" I could almost hear the antennae erupt from Belinda's hair.

Busted.

"I dropped by her place for an early cup of questionable coffee," I hedged. "She must have gone to the Belinda Clark School of Caffeination."

I planned my escape. "Come into my office, partner. I have a story to tell you."

Dennis likes to lead, not follow, but he loves apple fritters. Belinda let my bait and switch pass. She settled back into her chair with uncharacteristic self-restraint.

He called dibs on my desk chair. I handed him his treats and sank carefully into the sofa.

"I could have told you that Belinda already filled me in about the young man who came in Wednesday but you might have kept all the drinkable coffee for yourself. By the way, she feels guilty about scheduling what looks like another rough one without checking in with you first."

Taking a sip, his face registered ecstasy. "Almost as good as the taste of gin, before alcohol and cocaine tried to ruin my life." Dennis had his own special language for addiction and sobriety. "And." He looked at his wristwatch. "Since it's been more than eight hours since you spoke to her and I noticed the way you sat down on the couch, I'm sure there's more mayhem to report."

Between bites and sips, I reviewed the late breaking details about The Scholars of Calm, right up to the news of my road incident and Phil's call. I left out my interlude with Jill and made it clear I had no issue with Belinda. No one could have anticipated my new client's story would include cults and, unless I'd misread Phil's non-answer, a murder. Most important, no one close to me was likely to be surprised I'd found myself in the middle of another complicated case.

Dennis frowned at his last bite of pastry. "What the hell are we dealing with this time, Marlowe?"

We.

I was saved from my complete lack of an answer by Belinda at my doorway. "You both have clients, gentlemen." She gave me the look that my dad calls, "a mother's natural lie-detector." I handed her the last fritter. "Jill and early coffee. Really?"

Dennis stood with an accusing forefinger pointed my way. "More on this later."

Belinda's finger came next. "Yes. Later."

"I guess you're working through your guilt," he said to her.

"Indeed," I agreed, convinced we were intermingling topics about my life.

She gave us the suggestion of a smile. "I don't know how I put up with you two."

We didn't know either.

Dennis invited his client into his office and, cup in hand, I ushered Alicia into session. A super-charged seventy-two year old, Alicia found me while in the throes of a post-surgery depression. Her work included a struggle to decide whether to relate to me as her therapist or her son.

"I hope you're not drinking too much coffee, Hank."

"I'm also taking my vitamins and getting plenty of rest, Alicia."

"You're on to me," she said. "A fussy old control freak."

Alicia was a great deal more. She devoted her impressive life to the well-being of others. Director of a local nonprofit agency. Immigration rights advocate. Adoptive parent. Doting grandmother. In what she called her spare time she volunteered at a local food pantry. I saw her as an unsung heroine who had seen much, done much, and grown comfortable in her skin.

Within weeks of our first appointment, Alicia had bounced back to her energetic self, as she processed the fear and frustration of age as a factor in her recovery. In what might have been our final hour, though, an issue sitting below the surface found air.

"It's the first time I've given serious thought to retirement," she said. "It could be time. There are people I've prepared to take over. Good people."

Tears leaked from her eyes. She wiped them with the back of her hand. "But what's next? Golf? Gardening? God save me."

Time to wander into new territory.

"How about the younger woman who asked you for a date?" Early in our work I found Alicia had a wonderfully dry sense of humor. She'd told me about meeting a woman at a charity event, who followed her around all evening, then asked her out for a drink. The woman was sixty-seven.

A youngster's grin betrayed her. "I haven't had a date in fifteen years. What would I do with some wet-behind-the-ears kid."

Don't take the bait.

"What would be on your list?"

"Go on the tour of Greece I've put off forever. Push through my idea for starting home delivery at the food pantry. Eat more onion rings. Dip into the Jamaican rum I've been waiting to open for a special occasion."

She turned to my window, reviewing the past, envisioning the future, the light in her eyes giving me a glimpse of the unlined face of a girl with technicolor dreams and a turbo engine for a heart. "I took the quote you paraphrased from Victor Frankl in our last session, wrote it on a post-it and stuck in on my computer screen. It's been like a velvet hammer."

Victor. My hero.

"Ultimately, woman should not ask what the meaning of her life is, but rather she must recognize that it is she who is asked." She turned back. "I'm a believer. Do you know what really annoys me about all of this?"

Yes, I do.

"What really annoys you?"

"The damn surgery sparked something in me. It's time for a change."

"Because?"

"Because you and Victor asked the right questions and I'm interested in the answers." She smacked her palm on the chair's armrest for punctuation and looked at her watch.

"Enough for today?"

She gave me a grave look and stood.

Fake.

"I have a call to make," she said.

Time to take the bait.

"A call?"

She blessed me with another smile, that of a seeker to whom the next bend in her winding journey had been revealed. "To schedule a drink with a new friend." She reached out, shook my hand and opened the door. "Thanks. You've been more helpful than I imagined possible. I'll get back to you if I hit a stuck place."

And she was gone. For now. Therapy often works that way. Folks make changes. Take breaks. Return for another round.

Like life.

My wounded legs were stiff and I was tired. It takes extra energy to concentrate and manage pain simultaneously.

Water and a breath of fresh air. To balance the caffeine.

I almost made it out of my chair before Belinda resumed her post in my doorway. "Detective Evans is here."

Phil stood behind Belinda, towering over her, his buttoned-down appearance marred by the sag of fatigue.

My own fatigue was replaced with dread.

"We haven't found Seth. Yet." He anticipated my first question. "I wanted to give all of you a face-to-face update. Can we have everybody sit in on this, Belinda?"

"Everybody?"

"We have a missing persons enquiry related to Hank's client. Since any of you could pick up a call pertinent to our investigation, I want to cover the particulars with your team." He gave her room. "Plus, I know Hank will tell the whole story to Dennis and you as soon as I leave. Saves us all time."

"Oh Phillip." She moved toward Dennis' office, talking more to herself than us. "I'll see if he finished with his client. Missing people. Again?"

Phil sat, rested his fedora on the cushions, and, in an unusual show of vulnerability, tried to rub the weariness from his eyes. Dennis powered in my door with Belinda on his heels. I held my hand out before he launched into whatever questions he found most crucial. They sat. Phil pulled a cop noir spiral notepad from the pocket of his butterscotch camel sport coat. He tapped the pad on his knee and started with the most recent bad news.

"No one matching Seth's description got off the bus from Des Moines to Denver yesterday. We're working on both ends to find out who bought the ticket. We have an all points out in Iowa, Nebraska, and Colorado."

"How could this child fall through the cracks, Detective?" Belinda's frustration landed heavy. Seth was someone's child and she was a mother.

"Communication gaps and assumptions, Belinda," he said. "The university thought Seth had gone home for the summer and dropped out. That's not unusual. There are plenty of students who don't return without notifying the school. From Seth's report to Hank, he and his friends were encouraged to write their families and tell them things were going well, which bought The Scholars for Calm more time. Further into the summer, parents began contacting various local police departments to report that their kids had not returned home as expected. The website that was providing the day-to-day activities of the conference had been taken down and they were unable to reach their sons and daughters by phone. The students are from all over the country. No one realized that a group from the same university were somewhere in Iowa until Seth ended up in Hank's office and we initiated our investigation."

I had questions, but Phil opened his notepad and pressed on.

"We ran the plates on the pickup truck and van. They're registered to a man in Billings, Montana, the owner of a fleet of vehicles in various stages of restoration. He has never owned a pickup or a van, but did have the plates of numerous vehicles stolen in the past year."

"Numerous?" Dennis was into precision.

"He couldn't give Dale the exact number of cars he has on his property. Apparently they fill a sizable acreage." Detective Dale Goodman was Phil's partner and my self-appointed nemesis. I visualized the man testing the outer edges of Goodman's meager patience.

"I'm guessing the guy never reported the thefts to the police," Dennis said.

"No he did not." Phil continued. "We rushed the toxicology and prints on the man known as Lawrence. He had a record. Carlos Musslewhite, career scam artist. The findings included a far beyond therapeutic combination of opioids, benzodiazepines, and stimulants." His face betrayed—never believe you've heard it all. "Laced with a toxic weed killer. The forensic team found powder residue with traces of the toxin on a nightstand and in several of the numerous baggies of legal medications and illegal drugs lying on the floor. They also found an open container of the weed killer in the barn."

"You're telling us this Musslewhite decided to up his high on a cocktail of benzos, speed, and lethal garden chemicals?" Dennis stopped himself. "Sorry, folks. That was cruel."

"An important question, though," Phil said. "It has been established, based on previous arrests, that Carlos was a known drug user. We got a partial print from the container of weed killer, missed when somebody wiped it down. It belongs to Kenton Braxton. He and Musslewhite were partners in an insurance scam on senior citizens in Colorado. They did time together and jumped parole more than a year ago."

I had the next obvious question. "How did this guy's prints get on a canister of poison?"

Phil tossed his notepad on the sofa, an act of extreme frustration for the man. "I pulled up Braxton's picture. He was the man directing the kids in the phony hymn we heard at the farm."

"Not from another university," I said.

"No. An associate of Musslewhite's. It appears that Braxton, for reasons unknown, added an odorless weed killer from the stash of garden supplies to the drugs Musslewhite was ingesting. On its own, each dose would have made him increasingly sick. Mixed with the other drugs, snorting magnified the impact. In lay terms, his heart and lungs shut down."

"Oh my." Belinda spoke for all of us.

"We believe Braxton then packed the kids into the van Hank and I saw in the pole barn and took them God knows where. We have no idea if Seth is still with them." He looked up, as if a higher power might help him nail down their location. "They were fast. The house was a mess."

"I'm missing something else here." Dennis' said. "As the saying goes, we need a motive."

"Seth told Hank his parents run a construction business. We now know the families we have located are all wealthy. The Scholars of Calm targeted these kids. Lonely and rich." Phil rubbed the fingers on his right hand together in the universal sign for cash. "Money is in the equation."

Phil stowed the pad in his jacket and collected his hat. "I need to, I will find where they've taken the students. Dale is working on fingerprints. They're all over the house and gardening tools. Maybe we'll get a hit on someone else we can track. We've tapped into all nationwide missing persons databases."

I grabbed a legal tablet from my desk and started writing down the moves Phil was making. I wanted to remember and it was the closest I could get to doing something useful.

"This has crossed state lines," he said. "The Colorado Bureau of Investigation is being read in to help us pin down the backstory of Taranis, who seems to operate completely underground."

Phil stopped. It was the greatest volume of words I'd ever heard him speak in one sitting. He blew a deep breath from the cavern in his chest, hesitated like a man preparing to lift an oppressive weight, and pushed his bulk off the sofa.

"By the way, Hank. We didn't find an SUV when we searched the farm. But, at this time, we have no idea how many vehicles they might have stashed." I watched him do his best to square his shoulders and paint a look of confidence on his face. "We know they are on the run. Be alert and please use all available security measures. If you see anything or anyone suspicious, call 911, then call me. If you hear from any of the involved parties, call me. I'll let you know when I find the group."

I. Not we. When. Not if.

He nodded his head in deference to Belinda. She caught my eye and tilted her head toward the exit. I caught up to him in the hallway.

"Hank." I could hear another apology coming my way.

"Detective Evans." I made a weak stab at humor. "If I could reach high enough, I'd rest my hand on your shoulder. But I'm short and my arm hurts. If I can help, I'm all the way in on this with you."

"That's part of what concerns me."

Here it comes.

"I'm an experienced police officer, who's made serious mistakes on this case." The man was a pillar of honesty. "You are not a detective."

"True."

"There are some very bad people involved. I do not yet know how many, or where they are."

I.

"So please accept this in the spirit it is intended." I made no promises, so he kept talking. "I am certain of three things about you."

First finger.

"You are a skilled therapist."

Second finger.

"You have a big heart."

Third.

"This is exactly the kind of hornet's nest you insert yourself into."

Dad would say I arrived in this world with a "leap before you look" approach to hazard warnings.

"You have me there, Phil. But, here are a couple more facts. I got to this mess first. Seth was my client before he was your case. A case that is being run by a detective who, for reasons I have yet to determine, is getting caught up in another personal, not purely professional, agenda."

I knew Phil understood my reference, a memory shared from the early days of our friendship.

"I hear you." His face registered annoyance and acceptance in rapid succession. "I guess we'll have to keep an eye on one another." He settled his fedora on his head.

"I do insist that you remember what happened the last time you played amateur PI."

Favoring the big man with the last word, I watched his stride consume the yardage to the stairwell. He hadn't filled in the blanks, but he had confirmed my suspicions.

Not for the first time, I was struck by our similarities. Size differential, race, religion, and career choice aside, Phil and I were some archetypal version of the same guy.

An overdeveloped sense of duty fed by a mixed bag of motivations. The Jungian experts on Shadow would have a field day with us.

I stared down the empty hall.

Two sets of eyes are unlikely to be enough for this one.

The ringing of our landline got my attention.

"Anderson & Greenberg Counseling, this is Belinda. Yes, he's available. Please hold. Hank!"

I hurried into the office.

"It's Seth! Line one."

Waggling my finger at Dennis and Belinda, I got to my desk and grabbed the handset. Making myself sit, I hit the blinking red button.

Calm and easy.

"This is Hank."

"This is Seth." His voice trembled. "Do you remember me, Mr. Anderson?"

"I sure do, Seth. Are you safe? In a safe place?"

"Yes. I had to rest. I'm scared. I feel better and not good at the same time."

I reached for a pen and scratch pad. "What's better, Seth?" I wrote CATCH PHIL and passed the pad to Dennis. He ran.

"I got more sleep, which was nice." He sounded slightly less spacey. "My brain isn't as foggy and I didn't have any dreams about hurting people. But, my hands are shaky and I'm sweating a lot, even though I'm cold. I'm still really tired."

I paired the information we'd been given by Phil with Seth's new symptoms.

The after-effects of his ordeal. And withdrawal. Dosed with Musslewhite's personal chemistry set. Pre-weed killer?

"How's your breathing feel?"

"The burrito upset my stomach, but it sure was good."

Tangential thoughts.

"Are you drinking plenty of liquids?"

"Lots of water. I had a couple of root beers from the machine."

"Where are..."

"I'm really sorry, Mr. Anderson."

Dennis rushed in the door and pushed the pad in front of me.

PHIL'S GONE. CALLED HIM. ON HIS WAY BACK.

"Sorry about what, Seth?"

"I took some of his money. And a phone."

"Whose money?"

"Lawrence's. He picked me up after our meeting. I told him I felt better. He didn't want to talk to you."

Of course not.

"When we got back to camp, he let me sleep. After I woke up he said I had a special assignment. Lawrence said we were going to have the Feast of Awakening. It was still dark. Brother Theodore took me to the creek and left. To fish. I like to fish, Mr. Anderson." His thoughts wandered away. "In the mountains."

"Seth."

"I miss my family. I want to go home."

Keep up, Anderson.

"I'll help you get home, Seth."

"The fish weren't biting." His distress catapulted him back to the story. "I fished for a long time, but nobody came for me. I got lost in the woods. I was so tired. I fell asleep under a tree. Man, the bugs were still biting."

"How about we…"

"I walked for a long time, Mr. Anderson."

"Where are you now, Seth?"

"Everybody left me." My question was getting buried under his confusion. "I went upstairs, even though

Lawrence told us it was his sacred space. His door was open. He was on the bed. I think he was dead." His words came faster. "There was blood all over his face and pills everywhere and the keys to the truck and money laying on the dresser. I'm so sorry." An eruption of sobs muffled his apology. "I took the keys and some money. I was going to get help. But I was so scared. I took the truck. After I ate I slept for a long time."

"You needed to sleep."

"I want to go home. I'll pay back the money."

Ground him in something familiar and safe.

"Have you called your parents, Seth?"

"I tried. OVER AND OVER! I keep getting wrong numbers."

Wrong choice. Short-term memory lapses.

"I found your card in my pants." His breath starting coming in spurts, like a child waking from night terrors. "I called you."

"Good thinking. Very good thinking."

I heard bed springs squeak. He took a deep breath and sniffled into the phone. "Thank you. Was I right? Is Lawrence dead?" His thoughts jumped another random hurdle.

"Let's concentrate on getting you home, Seth. Where are…"

"He is!" Dodging the question detonated his terror. "Ohhhhh!"

The line went dead.

"Seth?" I had my finger on redial when Phil jogged through the door. "He panicked and hung up. I blew it when he asked about Lawrence."

"Is he safe?"

"Yes."

"How about a location?"

"We didn't get that far."

"Was he alone?"

"He said I, not we, when he talked about leaving the camp."

"With your permission, we'll trace the call."

"Definitely. I don't know if I kept him on long enough."

"Not a problem. I'll get back to you when I know more." He abruptly left the way he came, pulling the door to our suite behind him. I sat back, uncharacteristically speechless.

"Apparently we're out of the loop," Dennis said.

"Redial," Belinda instructed. I checked the caller ID and followed orders.

You've reached Marcel. Leave your message.

I made four attempts. The greeting didn't change.

"Now what?" My answer came in the form of my next client walking in the door.

"We go back to work," Belinda announced, then whispered. "Until we hear good news from Phillip."

Something we all could agree on.

An essential part of therapy is shifting attention from the previous client's struggles to the next important person in the door. I spent the rest of the day drifting to concerns about Seth and his friends between sessions, reeling myself back for the work at hand, slip sliding away, and so forth. I pushed myself to focus on the underlying depression Cleo encountered after her first year of sobriety, followed by an hour of pre-marital counseling with Barry and Sonya. My afternoon finished with Sam, cautiously optimistic after interrupting years of cyclical, shame-based sexual acting out, an underserved area of struggle that continued to find its way into my practice.

As I tidied up my ever-present antagonist, paperwork, my stomach reminded me that a breakfast of fritters topped with worry didn't measure up to a balanced diet.

You're supposed to be a role model for health, Anderson.

I've been told that soldiers in combat situations are advised, sleep when you can, you don't know when you'll have another chance. I substituted therapist for soldier and eat for sleep, images of a serious takeout order from my new favorite Kosher deli rising up. My short-lived brush with comfort was suspended in mid-step by two somber expressions commanding the waiting room. Belinda's was all too recognizable; we'd navigated a few calamities together. The second belonged to the woman standing ramrod straight at her side.

Oh no.

"Catherine?"

"Phillip has not called all day." Like Belinda, Phil's wife preferred the formal of his given name. The agony in her measured tone was stark against her rigid posture and prayerful hands. "It's a ritual. He calls me when he gets a free moment." She held her hand up, knowing what I would say next. "He calls, without fail."

"He didn't pick up when you called him." I knew she would have tried.

"He did not." Her hand went to her mouth, as if she could hold in her disbelief. "I left the office as soon as possible and went home." Catherine was the director of a nonprofit accounting firm assisting startups and small businesses in economically distressed parts of the state. "I thought he might be under the weather and didn't want to bother me. You know how he is." She stopped short of a lecture on the big man's rub dirt on it and get back on the field work ethic. "But, his police vehicle is parked in front of the house. His personal car is gone from the garage. That never happens."

She rocked on her heels. Belinda placed a hand on her elbow and guided her into the desk chair. "He left a message." She reached out and I took a page torn from his notepad:

Catherine, I'm on the way to find the young man and other children. Give the kids a hug for me. Please let them know I'm working this weekend. I'll see you soon. Love

The note answered my next question. Why had Catherine come to me instead of contacting his department? I replayed the memory I'd confronted Phil with a few hours earlier:

Phil and I had known one another for less than a year. I'd only met Catherine in passing.

She opened her call with, "Thank you for everything you did to help Sasha." I'd counseled a church member for an adjusted fee, a person who needed mental health services, not incarceration, for a minor offense.

"I'm glad I could help."

I let her take the time she needed to arrive at the real reason she called. She offered me an out.

"I know we just met. I don't want to be a bother."

"No bother, Catherine."

"Have you heard about the Bushman case?"

I had. The local media was all over the story of Brother Conrad Abraham Bushman, a tent preacher in the county. He'd recently initiated a custody battle with one of his cousins, a former member of the flock who fled to the city with his family, away from the Brother's dubious theology and apparent desire to control the finances of all parishioners. In his extraordinarily vain effort to gain custody of the cousin's children on religious grounds, it became apparent to the court that the sanctimonious Brother Bushman had multiple wives, something frowned upon by the Iowa legal system.

"How does this involve Phil?"

"He and Detective Goodman were assigned to investigate the bigamy charge." She hesitated, like clients who ask for my help, then wonder if it was a mistake to open the door to their story.

She decided.

"I'm afraid Phillip has appointed himself to the task of ruining this man's life." Her voice gained strength as she named her worry. "He isn't sleeping well. He leaves early, comes home late. He isn't tuned into the kids, which is very unusual."

I'd learned that Lucas and Maggie were Phil's greatest joy.

"He shows up at the Brother's tent meetings. On his own. He stands in the back. As you know, he would be hard to miss in a bunch of white people who aren't six foot five." We would have laughed if her fear hadn't been so urgent. "He sits in his car outside the man's home, making sure to be seen as this false prophet's flock comes and goes."

No doubts where Catherine stood with regard to the Brother.

"How do you know this?"

"Like Phillip, I have my sources." It struck me that Detective Dale Goodman, who held a deep admiration for his partner and a total disrespect for me, had squealed on Phil. He was probably keeping track of his friend and reported in to Catherine in an effort to short-circuit official action that could torpedo Phil's career.

"How can I help?"

Having been told by my new friend that his wife was, like himself, a by-the-numbers kind of person, I imagined she had a plan.

She did.

An intimate family and friend intervention at the Evans home took place the next evening. Catherine, Dale Goodman, and myself. Goodman and I put aside our blossoming hostility for the job at hand. The kids were sent to play at the neighbor's house. The adults were sitting in the kitchen when Phil got home, late. There was no small talk. Catherine brought coffee. Phil sat and stared through the wall.

I was invited to speak first. I told Phil he looked done in, like he'd been drug through a keyhole sideways. I emphasized his dedication to family and the job as the cornerstones of my respect for him. In an attempt to penetrate his reserve, I unabashedly played the guilt card, detailing how his off-the-book behavior could damage everyone and everything he loved.

His initial response, I had yet to learn, was Phil's standard MO in tough emotional situations. His deadpanned stare probably scared the hell out of criminals. It worked on me. Mixed with the underlying menace of a wounded combatant returned from a deadly battle that radiated from him, I sipped my drink and settled in for a slow and uncertain outcome.

Goodman said little. Ordinarily a man who loved to run his mouth, the misery imprinted on his face spoke volumes. He simply told Phil he had his partner's back.

It was Catherine who took us the rest of the way. She wasn't a tall woman. I pictured Phil leaning down to kiss her goodbye in the morning and hello at night. However, regal was not too precious a word for the strength she projected. Goodman and I were the supporting cast, Dale, his loyal partner and me, an outsider who could hold a confidence. We nodded our heads in rhythm, hanging on her every word.

Catherine reminded Phil of how much she loved his devotion to making the world a safe place for children and families. She told him she understood his rage and his bone-deep desire for justice. She reminded him he had done all he could do for Matthew.

Matthew? I looked at Goodman, who shrugged his own confusion.

Catherine finished by calling upon Phil to remember he was not God, he was of God, and professed to believe in God's plan. Even when he didn't fully comprehend the blueprint.

Phil didn't cry. He didn't collapse into a profession of the faith he and Catherine embraced as their path through life. He didn't tell stories from a past that was clearly a driving force in his recent behavior. He simply took his wife's hand and reinstalled the Phil I was becoming familiar with, the threat in his eyes wiped clean by the force of her love.

"Time to stop and let our system work," he said, like this was what we needed to understand. "Dale. Hank. Thank you for your friendship."

Goodman and I got up in concert, aware we'd been dismissed. We left in separate cars, never again to mention the meeting.

On the way home that night, I realized that Catherine had invited us to spark Phil's discomfort, allowing her to confront him out of the spotlight of the department. At the conclusion, pleased with the result, she allowed him to have the final word, to save face. I also reflected on a new understanding of the two sonic forces that fed Phil's pledge to protect and serve.

Love and pain.

Pretty common for people seeking to forge a better world.

Unknowingly, Brother Bushman had violated our detective's moral code in ways both vile and personal. As the case evolved, I came to believe that the jail time the sham clergyman served for fraud, tax evasion, and bigamy was a walk in the park compared to the injury he might have sustained if not for the intercession of Catherine Evans.

I was also left with questions.

Who was Matthew and what happened?

"I don't want to be a bother." She'd already replayed the same memory.

"I'm glad you came to us." Belinda said. "How can we help?"

The tears rolled free-form down her cheeks, her eyes full of questions.

This time, she has no plan.

"I'll call him," I said. "With your permission, I'll call Goodman."

"Of course."

Then I said something therapists are not supposed to say. "I promise we will take care of this."

She stood and wiped her tears with a tissue offered by Belinda. Smoothing her unwrinkled cardigan with both hands, she hugged our office manager as if she was the one who needed consoling, and closed the space between us with renewed energy.

Their kids probably stride briskly into school every morning

"Hank." She stopped within reach. "I've been a police officer's wife for a long time. I do know one thing. We're going into the weekend. My Phillip is off the rotation and believes he has several days to do whatever he is planning to do without close supervision or reprimand from his commander. He probably thinks he will wrap up this case and be back in his office by Monday morning. He is not always as humble as he should be."

Too gracious to say, like you, Hank.

"But he is a wonderful judge of loyalty and friendship." She laid her hand on my arm. "He trusts you. So, I trust you."

No pressure there.

"I need to get home. To keep things normal." She turned to Belinda. "You're a mother. You understand."

"I do. Take care, dear."

Out the door she went, to do what spouses and partners of police officers have done for centuries. Try to keep things normal. Contain the worry. Hold down the fort.

Belinda let the hush settle before speaking. "There's a back story."

She didn't know about Brother Bushman, but she did pay attention.

"Yep."

"How did it turn out?"

"Poorly for the fool who crossed Phil's path. Better for Phil than it would have if Catherine had not intervened."

"Now what?"

"Obviously I find Phil and bring him home."

"Obviously. How?"

"At this point, I have no clear strategy."

"Nothing unusual there. Thinking as you go is what you do." I heard both encouragement and caution in my guardian angel's declaration. "Get to it then."

I stepped back into my office and saw the usual mess on my desk was overshadowed by an aggressive dot flashing on my cell phone screen. I did the techno face recognition unlock thing and played the voicemail.

"This is Phil," he rumbled.

Like I wouldn't recognize your voice.

"I'm on the way to find Seth and track the other kids. I've got some ideas about the direction this is headed. I need you to stay in Des Moines. If you hear from Seth again, find out where he is and call me." The message was disrupted by the muffled noise of a truck passing at interstate speed. "Keep Dale in the loop. Try not to antagonize him." His words lacked their usual authoritative muscle. "Try not to constantly antagonize him."

End of message.

This is bad.

Phil had gone solo. This time, in search of young people to save. And, I was certain, in search of bad people to hurt.

I was getting tired of being hung up on, so I called Catherine. She answered from her car and pulled over. I gave her Phil's message, word for word, including the piece I'd left out of our first conversation, her husband's quick exit after gaining permission to track my client's call.

"What am I missing here, Catherine?" Intuition told me I'd been denied the full explanation for my friend's anomalous behavior.

"He's such a good husband and father. But he keeps a lot inside."

No mental health training required to suss that out.

"You might remember I spoke of Matthew when the Brother so-and-so situation came up."

"I do."

"As I said, he trusts you. But he stopped talking about his little brother's death a long time ago. Even with me."

The line crackled with heartache as she went deeper into the story of Phil's loss of perspective:

Matthew was, in many ways, the polar-opposite of Phil. Undersized. Outspoken. Moving through their childhood like he always had somewhere else to be, he regularly stirred the pot to see if he could make something interesting happen. Phil was the big brother, numerically and physically. He protected Matthew from schoolyard bullies. Sometimes he protected him from his own carelessness.

And he was almost within reach when the branch Matthew balanced on cracked and he plunged from the upper reaches of the oak climbing tree to the pavement-like dirt patch below. First on the scene, two police officers did everything possible within their limited training in catastrophic injuries until the ambulance arrived. It wasn't enough.

Matthew had been ten years old. Phil was fourteen. Their parents immersed the family in their faith. They grieved and spoke often of Matthew, with love and humor and frustration. No one blamed Phil. Except Phil.

Unknown to anyone but Catherine, who met her husband-to-be a savagely painful six years later, Phil devoted his life to his brother's memory. He excelled academically. He achieved as a shot putter at Roosevelt High School. He worked weekends in the summer, as a lifeguard. A scholarship athlete to the University of Northern Iowa, he completed a bachelor's degree in criminal justice and enrolled in the Des Moines Police Academy.

Catherine vividly recalled his graduation at the top of the training class, accepting that Phil, and by proxy and love, herself, had signed up for a long journey of service and sorrow.

Phil had a brother.

"So you see, Hank. As steady as my Phillip is, certain cases grab ahold of him."

Like a lot of cops. And therapists.

"It also explains why he's so protective of me."

"Yes. I believe you remind him of Matthew."

Hank Anderson, psychological cliché.

"I have a pretty good idea where he's headed," I continued.

"So, you'll have Dale find him."

"Yes," I lied.

"And you'll keep me updated."

"Yes." It was tough to double down on deceiving this wonderful woman.

"Then I will let you go. Thank you for listening."

I hung up the phone and sat still. No lightning. No thunder. I touched my sore face, arm, and knees. I hadn't been struck down by the gods for my deception.

Maybe doing good work for good people counterbalances deliberate lies.

I grabbed my briefcase and went for the door before the gods changed their minds.

"You'll update us, soon and often." Belinda yelled at my back.

"Of course."

"Liar."

I skidded to a halt.

"Don't give me any of your fibs about keeping us in the loop, mister." She aimed the deadly trigger finger at me. "Whatever you get up to, stay in contact, or I will personally track you down and rain hellfire and damnation upon your foolish self." The incongruent tapestry of loving mother and Old Testament havoc was a unified truth in the world according to Belinda.

Fibs? Nobody uses that word anymore. She does channel Mom.

"I understand." We both knew I did. We both knew it might not matter.

I hustled into the hall at the exact moment Dennis came out of the elevator, fresh from teaching a seminar on Motivational Interviewing at a local treatment center. He was adjusting his practice toward consultation after several decades as the go-to addictions therapist in Des Moines.

"Where you headed?"

"I don't have time to stop and explain."

He reversed course and pushed the L button, sidestepping my effort to avoid his input. The sluggish elevator gave me enough time to hit the highlights of my conversations with Catherine before we made it to the lobby. I had no expectation this would satisfy him.

Into the parking lot we went.

"Who's your client, Marlowe?"

"Seth."

"Not Phil. Not Catherine. Not the other lost kids."

I wanted to argue with him.

"No."

"Are you a cop?"

"I already had this conversation with Phil. Is that it?"

"Of course not." He put his hand on my chest, then his own. "You and I tripped over these questions in the not-too-distant past. You went way too far and I was right behind you."

"Indeed." His reminder brought me out of the tunnel of my misplaced anger.

"It's a miracle that we, and two other men we love, are upright and alive today. Remember my questions. Remember your answers." He voice softened. "I know where your heart is at. You've just learned of Phil's loss." He gave me space. "When the time is right, he'll turn to you."

"Not today," I said. Dennis often led me where I needed to go.

"Not today. Now, get rolling and call Goodman. Give this mess to him. He may be a jerk, but he's our jerk. And he is a cop."

The Jeep made its way home with minimal guidance. Even in my distracted state, I noticed the tunnel of maples on our narrow street making their gradual passage from vivid green to fiery red. I dismissed the notion of not finding Seth before they became brown and floated to the ground.

My next visual was a pale silver car sitting in front of our brick-and-stucco home, sending a twitch into my right eye. Unexpected vehicles still triggered memories of bad guys invading the Hank and Haley safe space. James had installed every form of alarm known to anyone not working for the CIA. Over time, the intrusive thoughts had quieted.

Until yesterday's run-in with the black SUV.

I slowed and drifted through the tight spot between the characterless sedan and my cross-street neighbor Ed's retro Thunderbird. A full moon face appeared in the driver's window to my left.

Goodman.

The typical impact of seeing Phil's partner was annoyance. Today, I carried Dennis' dictate and the notion that the man might have important news. By the time I stepped into the driveway he'd hauled himself from behind the wheel. His suit looked like it had been slept in, his face a mishmash of hyper alert and groggy.

"We need to talk, Anderson."

"Come inside. You look like you could use a cup of coffee."

He trailed me in the door. I grabbed the supplies for the most useful piece of equipment in my life, a twelve-cup Cuisinart, and set to work on caffeine prep, giving room for the detective to squeeze by into my compact kitchen. He found his way to a stool, rested his elbows on the countertop, and cracked his neck. I busied myself with cups, no cream or sugar. I didn't like the guy, but I appreciated whatever baggage he carried that was heavy enough to force him to my door.

The pot gurgled complete. I filled two mugs and placed one on the breakfast bar in front of him. I stayed on my feet, concentrating on a speck of worn paint on the cabinet next to him. He reached for the coffee, took a couple of scalding hot sips, and swiveled my way.

"I'm going to say a few things. I don't want you to ask questions or interrupt. Can you do that?"

"Sure."

He nodded.

"I know we don't like each other."

Agreed.

"I give you a hard time. Mostly, I'm a hard guy." I fought off another jab of agreement.

"Not when it comes to Phil and his family." His downed more coffee. "Back before you started coming around, I was going through a bad stretch. My wife was sick. We don't, didn't have any kids. Josie and the job. That was my world."

His sorrow filled the space.

"She died. It was slow and it was horrible. She was my best friend and I wouldn't wish what she went through on my worst enemy." He stopped to stare into his mug, as if it reflected how she suffered. "I started drinking more."

His eyes darted, daring me to speak. I kept my word.

"Phil and Catherine looked out for me. On work days he knocked on my door until I got up and cleaned up. On days off they both came to my door, took me out with their kids to Gray's Lake or the zoo. Sometimes we went to the Farmer's Market. Hell, they even got me to go to the Art Museum. They fed me." He patted his ample gut, a better reminiscence.

Here it comes.

"Phil took me to an open AA meeting. I kept going. I quit drinking. I've got almost six years sober. Then he sent me to a grief group at his church. The one he should have gone to himself."

He knows about Matthew.

He held his empty cup out for a free refill. I poured and he sipped loudly, releasing a heavy sigh. "I could not have dug out of that hole on my own. Phil was there for me. Every day until I started to become human again. Saved my job, maybe my life. I owe him." He pointed the mug at me. "You owe him, too. He saved your ass with those DEA characters after that Jensen cluster..." He skipped the colorful conclusion. "He made it sound simple. It wasn't. You have no idea how he went to the mat for you."

Like Phil not to tell me.

"So, here's how you and I set it right. We find Phil 'cause he won't return my calls. We help him with whatever lone crusade he signed up for this time." He slid his mug across the counter for another refill. "The lieutenant who heads up missing persons is my second cousin. He cleared me for the weekend to work this. Grab an extra pair of clean undies and your tooth brush and we're out of here."

I poured a third round.

"My turn," I said.

"I knew this was a mistake." He came to his feet and reached to brush me aside. "Forget I asked."

"Sit down." I blocked his retreat. "I listened to you. Now I've got two questions."

His laughter was packed with hostility. "You gonna stop me from leaving, Anderson?"

I ignored the obvious answer. "Who put you up to this? There is no way you decide on your own to come here and ask for my help."

Sheepish is the word that came to mind for the hard-nosed detective's next expression. He didn't sit, but he retreated.

"Catherine called. She told me she'd been to see you." His face softened when he mentioned her name. "Her exact words were, Dale, on further reflection, I'm concerned Hank was less than fully honest with me."

Didn't come close to fooling her.

"She was afraid you might not keep your promise to reach out to me and, instead, go off on another one of your half-cocked rescue operations. Then I'd have to figure out how to clean up after both you and Phil."

"That last part would be your exact words, not hers."

"Right."

"She asked you to find me, ask for my help, and keep me out of serious trouble while helping Phil keep out of serious trouble."

"Pretty much," he admitted. "Next question."

"How do we find Phil?"

"Fair enough," he said. "I have someone tracking Seth's call to you, too."

"More intel from Catherine."

"She's all in on protecting Phil from himself," he said. "I haven't heard back from my guy yet, but we're heading west."

"West?"

"A confused, frightened kid from Colorado with wheels who wants to go home. Which direction does he go?"

"West."

"Best guess. By now Phil knows where the call originated. He's ahead of us and I'm counting on him to head that direction, too."

"Okay." I turned the coffee maker off. "I'm in."

"That's it? No smart-ass remarks?"

"When you're right, you're right," I said, understanding that Goodman was about to put himself on the line for the Evans family and I was the clear, if unpleasant choice to go along for the ride. "It happens so seldom, I'm at a loss for words."

He grunted. "And I was nervous you were going to go all namby-pamby emotionally supportive on me."

I was searching for my next comeback when the side door rattled open and another unexpected visitor made his appearance, stepping slowly into the kitchen.

"Good to see you, Detective." Dad had the security codes and his own set of keys.

"Good to see you on your feet, Mr. Anderson." Goodman had history with my dad, too.

"Dad?"

"Even better to see you, Son."

When he hugged me, I saw the notation on the wall calendar. Dad was in Des Moines for a regional food and beverage convention. I'd invited him to stay with me and spend some quality time with his granddaughter.

"I completely forgot."

"Not a problem." His sturdy gaze moved from me to Goodman. "I do have a question, though. No offense intended, Detective, but I don't recall you two fellows spending a lot of time chatting over coffee. What brings you to my son's home?" Courteous. Direct.

Goodman gave Dad a real smile. "Sir, you may have a future in breaking criminals down."

"Years of listening to alcoholics flirt with honesty." Dad broke his own anonymity. "Plus, forty years of conversations with customers over cheeseburgers and root beer."

I was mystified. As close as Dad would come to bragging, fencing with a genuine compliment from the eternally acidic Goodman.

"It's J.R. to my friends," he added.

"Dale to mine, J.R."

What is happening?

It got quiet. This was Goodman's call.

"Police business, J.R. Your son is involved in a case that Phil Evans and I are on. I came to ask for Hank's help." He barely grimaced when he said—Hank's help. "I understand you and your son have plans, but I'd like to borrow him for a couple of days. Could you keep the home fires burning while he's working with us?"

"Now, Detective. I may have been born yesterday but I got up early to study."

"Yes, sir." Goodman gave a salute of respect. "Detective Evans is in some difficulty and, as hard as it is for me to admit, Sigmund Fraud may be of some assistance in the matter."

"A measure of balance has been restored to the universe," I said.

Dad lowered a small overnight bag to the floor. "Well, that takes the baloney out of the sandwich. Home fires it is, men."

I left the room marveling at my dad's ability to befriend wayward individuals of all shapes and sizes, validating the nickname I'd imposed on him: The Sage. Pulling my closet open, my injured arm reminded me that fast isn't always better. Jeans, t-shirts, hoodies, shaving kit, one set of casual business gear. And the clean underwear recommended by Goodman.

I took a beat to reflect on his story.

He doesn't dislike me. Somehow, my presence triggers the pain of his loss. He projects his vulnerability onto me. Or, he just dislikes me.

I shifted gears, practicing the argument I was certain to have with Dennis at a later date.

I was not meddling. Phil brought me deeper into this when he asked me to ride out to the camp with him. Catherine asked for my help. Goodman, who usually tells me to stay as far away from him as possible, wanted me on the job.

Maybe I'd be of some value in finding Seth safe and sound. Maybe I could repay a debt to a friend in trouble.

Maybe this is you rationalizing another of your ill-considered risks.

Since the argument was in my head, I won. I threw an extra pair of warm socks in the bag, just in case my logic was flawed.

Goodman stood in the kitchen with dad, holding a brown paper bag and a large thermos, pleasure plastered across his tired face.

"Look what your dad pulled out of his suitcase. J.R. brought cold chicken and potato salad from his restaurant." He raised the thermos with childlike joy. " It's root beer."

"Never go visiting with empty hands." I smiled at Dad.

Goodman opened the door. "I'll be in the car. Easy Does It, J.R."

AA slogan.

I embraced dad, swollen arm and all. "I can't leave you alone for two minutes."

"I find recovering alcoholics under every rock, Son. Lucky you."

When I released him, he held on tight.

Unsteady on his feet?

I had questions. He beat me to the punch.

"I trust you and Dale will do right by Phil. Three good men." He moved me to arms-length.

"Something you need to tell me, Dad?" My spidey-sense tingled.

"Nothing that can't wait until you get back."

I didn't like his answer. He gave me a tender shove toward the door.

"Haley's at home with Gail this weekend. Gail will remember you were coming. Give her a call, I'm sure she'd love to see you and free up time for you to enjoy the Haley Express."

"I'm on the job, Hank."

I wanted to say more. I wanted to insist he say more. He turned his back to tidy up the kitchen. I'd known him a long time. The subject was closed.

For now.

~~~

One hand on the steering wheel, Phil finished his message to Hank, thumbed disconnect, and slid his cell into the phone mount. He had never laid down a bet, but he knew the smart money was against the man following his directive and sticking close to home. It was more likely his friend was already concocting a list of justifications for injecting himself further into the search for Seth and the other students.

But, who was he to judge? Leaving a handwritten note for Catherine. Not returning Dale's calls. Circumventing the chain of command. Having no talent for self-deception, the best Phil could do was offer up his list of reasons for deliberately abandoning his post.

The clock was ticking. The Scholars of Calm had proven they saw people as expendable— they killed their own. He had no idea how many of them there were. He did know he had to find Seth before they did.

A text came through. He slowed and checked.

The trace.

Seth's call had originated from a motel in Avoca. At this speed, he could make be there in less than an hour.

~~~

Seth had no idea what the name of the town was, or the name of the motor lodge where he'd pulled off. Or how long he'd been passed out on the bed.

But he knew Lawrence was dead. He massaged his temples, letting the phone ring unanswered.

Light leaked through the edges of the blackout curtain on the lone window. Maybe fresh air would help. Palms on the mattress, he weaved to his feet. He stood flatfooted, legs wide apart, like a guy who couldn't hold his liquor. Opening the door, he squinted into the sun and almost walked into Emma's fist.

"Emma?" More confusion tumbled through him.

"I was getting ready to knock. It's good to see you, Seth!" She caressed his cheek with her fingertips, like she was amazed it was him. "I've been so worried about you." She held out a white paper bag and a soft drink cup. "I brought you a burger and a soda."

Seth leaned into the doorframe to steady himself. It seemed odd that Emma would show up at this place, but through his blurred power to reason, he couldn't grab ahold of why.

"Are you going to invite me in?"

"I'm sorry. Sure." He backtracked from the entry and sank onto the twin bed filling nearly half of the compact room.

"I knew you would be hungry and tired." She set the food and drink on an end table and made herself at home on the second bed.

"I'm sorry," he repeated. "I already ate." He held his gurgling stomach. "And drank too much soda. But I am still tired."

"That's fine." He missed the catch of annoyance in her response. "How about we both lay back and have a nap?"

Without hesitation, Seth stretched out on the lumpy, sunken mattress, resting on clouds in comparison to the sleeping bag on threadbare carpet at the farm house. He sighed. A nagging jab of vigilance passed through his scattered thoughts. Lawrence? He needed to ask her about Lawrence. He wasn't sure if he heard himself speak before his system shut down.

When he woke again, Seth wondered if Emma's appearance had been part of another dream. He looked at the other bed. It was empty. But the covers were a mess. A small grease-stained bag had tipped over on the end table. A full soda leaked condensation. There was a faint fragrance layered on the musty air.

Vanilla.

An exhale of relief that his imagination was not running amok gave him enough strength to pull upright on the bed, plant his feet on the floor, and stand. The earlier feeling that his head might roll off his shoulders had been replaced by the milder sensation of his brain slowly coming to rest in his skull.

Where had she gone?

He noticed the door was ajar. The murmur of a female in conversation seeped through the gap.

"Yes, I found him."

Emma. He reached to open the door.

"He's in Avoca. The tracker worked."

He stopped. He knew about trackers.

"No, I didn't get anything in him. He fell asleep." A pause. "Shut up." Her words were harsh, not the Emma he knew. "Stay on the back roads. I'm going to stash the truck. I'll get him to drink. Room 23. There's a manager in the office a few doors down. Don't park in front. You'll stand out. Call me when you get here."

Hearing the shuffle of shoes, a faraway, instinctual command urged him to move back onto the bed and mimic sleep. A rush of vanilla breeze came over him.

Emma was watching.

He was on the verge of nodding off one more time when he heard her step from carpet to pebbled concrete. She closed the door behind her, short of latching the automatic lock. He heard the metal-on-metal squeal of a truck door in need of lubricant change to the erratic rhythm of the worn engine and the crunch of tires over gravel as his ride faded into the distance.

"Emma is not a friend," he whispered to himself.

Seth still didn't understand what was happening, but something elemental had awakened in him. Eyes open, he got to his feet and gave his vision time to steady. He pulled a thin cotton blanket from the end of the bed and wrapped it around his shoulders in defense against the teeth-rattling shiver revisiting his body.

"Leave before she comes back. Don't drink the soda. Don't bring the phone."

He cracked the door and squeezed onto the uneven stoop, shading his eyes. The parking space in front of him was empty. He had to find another way home.

He looked right and headed into the neighborhoods.

~~~

The car was running when I opened the passenger door. Goodman's mouth was packed with chicken. He pointed, chewed, and sipped root beer from the thermos.

"Just throw your bag in the back seat."

"Geez. Close your mouth when you chew, Goodman." It worked.

Probably something his mom said, too.

I was surprised at the tidiness of the vehicle. I'd pegged Goodman for a stack of empty cup and burger containers on the floorboards kind of guy.

He licked his fingers and dropped the car into gear before I clicked my seatbelt. I salvaged a chicken leg and made short work of my favorite leftover. He hit the button on a mini-Bluetooth speaker hanging from the mirror and the willowy beauty of Elephant Revival, a band I still mourned, cued up. I let the fourth shock in the past ten minutes pass through me.

Loves Phil. AA. Gracious to Dad. Quality music. Maybe I've been teleported to an alternate universe.

We made our way through the neighborhoods. Past Ashworth Avenue, he pulled into a Casey's, went inside, and came out with a paper cup of coffee. He motioned me to come around, handing me the keys and the drink.

"You're going to drive so I can take a power nap."

"To where?"

He settled into the passenger seat and set his phone on the console.

"Like I said, west. Wake me if I don't hear the phone."

"One more question," I said.

"You're already annoying me."

"What if we drive all the way to Colorado and haven't found Seth or Phil?"

"I'm counting on Phil to make sure that doesn't happen."

Sounds like one of my plans.

"We're still on Daylight Savings Time, so we've got a little sun left. Keep it under a hundred, wild man, this is a personal vehicle."

He closed his eyes.

End of conversation.

～～

One could expect that any stranger wrapped in a blanket, meandering the side streets of a rural community of 1,500 would attract attention. Seth managed to cover a fair distance before another surge of exhaustion overwhelmed him, passing a gas station, a restaurant, and the public library before depositing himself on a wood slat bench in an empty, well-manicured park. He pulled the blanket snug and fell asleep. Dusk had activated the park's walkway light system by the time a couple exercising their German Shepherd shook his shoulder to make sure he was breathing, and called 911.

By the time the Avoca officer rolled up, Seth had befriended the dog and engaged the couple in pleasant, rambling conversation. It was easy for her to match the guy in the blanket with the missing person's report out of Des Moines. The officer thanked the locals and reported Seth Oberstreet as found and in protective custody. She asked for her sergeant and relayed the young man's disjointed story about a camp, a pickup truck, a dead man named Lawrence, and Emma, a woman who suddenly appeared at the door of his room on the edge of town.

The officer was instructed to transport Seth to the Avoca police station. Chief Hull arrived in street clothes to direct the action and locate the young man's family. An improvised task force was mustered and converged on the motel. The officers retrieved a phone, a bag of fast food, and a large cup of warm soda. The room was cordoned off. An investigative team from the sheriff's department was dispatched. An all-hands-on-deck canvassing of the area discovered an abandoned red pickup with Montana plates and up-to-date tags tucked behind a local auto repair. There was no sign of the young woman named Emma.

Several bottles of water, a stack of pancakes, and an emotional reunion call to his parents later, Seth was given a thorough once over by the on-call physician's assistant, who pronounced the young man shaken but medically stable. A rapid drug test was taken to confirm the provisional diagnosis that his jumbled thought process was, in part, the result of being several days clean from the diminishing effects of repeated low dose sedative ingestion administered without his knowledge. Seth's status was called into the Des Moines Police Department with the assurance that Avoca would see to his well-being until further informed. The lieutenant thanked the chief and gave him the phone number of a Detective Evans.

~~~

Phil was less than ten minutes from Avoca when the call came.

"This is Detective Evans."

"Detective. Chief Hull from Avoca. We found your guy."

A flood of gratitude woke Phil from the edge of highway hypnosis, right before it hit him that he'd been contacted by the Avoca Chief of Police, a man he'd never spoken to prior to this evening. He eased off the gas and took the exit south toward the township of Walnut, turning into an abandoned mini-mart. Avoiding a minefield of potholes, he parked next to a rusted-out flatbed trailer languishing on the gravel.

"How is he, Chief?"

"Confused, tired and hungry, but in one piece," he said. "He's guzzling water and eating everything we set in front of him. We tracked down the father's phone number and he's been in contact with his parents. The on-call physician's assistant from our town clinic gave him the once over. She believes he's several days into withdrawal from some type of sedative, administered without his consent."

Phil could hear a voice in the background.

"She says his vitals are strong and, for now, the treatment is rest, hydration, and emotional support."

"If she thinks he's up to it, I'd like to ask him a few questions."

"Hold on."

He heard a woman in the background say, "Keep it short."

"You get that, Detective?"

"I did."

"He's a little loose around the edges, but he has quite a story to tell about these Scholars of Calm people." The Chief clearly wanted Phil to hear he was in the know. "I'll put him on."

"Hello?"

"Seth, this is Detective Evans from the Des Moines Police Department."

"Hi."

"I'm mighty glad to hear you're safe, young man."

"Thank you. Do I know you?"

"I'm a friend of Hank Anderson's and we've been looking for you."

"Mr. Anderson. Oh my. I think I hung up on him. Is Lawrence really dead?"

"He is, Seth, but you had nothing to do with it." Phil spoke with gentle authority. "He had a medical problem. None of this is your fault. You are not in trouble and your only job is to rest up while we work on getting you home."

An explosion of breath came through the line.

"Seth. Can I ask you a question or two?"

"Anything."

"You told the officer that Emma came to your door at the motel."

"She wanted me to eat something, but I was full." He didn't need another question. "I fell asleep. When I woke up she was outside, talking on the phone. There was something about a tracker. She was mad and told somebody she was going to make me drink the soda."

"Did you hear the name of the person on the other end?"

"No. Then she left."

"Did you see her leave?"

"I heard her start the truck and drive away." Phil could almost hear the young man's cognitive cogs fighting to regenerate. "Which doesn't make sense. I gave the keys for the truck to the police." He sighed. "I'm really tired."

"Of course. You've been very helpful. You rest and I'll put my best people on getting you home."

"Thank you." The receiver clunked on a desk top.

"Detective."

Phil knew the chief had monitored the interview. "Chief."

"The lieutenant who gave me your number was vague about the particulars of this group of students you're searching for, not an unusual situation for us small town cops when dealing with you city people." Phil guessed it was Dale Goodman's uncle. "But, experience tells me he's covering somebody's tracks. Is there anything else I need to know?"

"Chief. On my own I've traveled well beyond the city limits in my search for Seth and the other students we believe have been kidnapped by a dangerous cult."

"Perhaps beyond a few other by-the-book limits, as well." The man had skills. "Thank you for your honesty, Detective. When you have your plan for getting young Oberstreet home, I'll be here."

Phil hung up, knowing he passed the chief's test, not knowing what the price of failure would have been. He also had a few more pieces of the puzzle in place, and a new set of questions.

No family had come forward to report a missing student with the first name, Emma. She was not a student. She was part of The Scholars. Emma tracked Seth to the motel, through the phone or a device on the truck. She moved the truck away from the motel to isolate him, thinking he'd still be asleep when she came back. Which meant she arrived in a third vehicle. She came alone and made a call. Which meant there was at least one crew member on the other end.

Braxton? On the move with the other students? Or, were there more like the two of them, hidden in the group? Or outside of the camp? Did they have a destination or were they simply on the run?

He was reaching for the ignition when his phone pinged. A text from Dale.

Anderson and I will meet you in Avoca.

Phil assumed the lieutenant had notified Dale of the call from Avoca. The anger Dale's message generated in him, proof of Hank's interference, clashed with his relief that the two men had formed some kind of unlikely partnership. He wasn't fond of conflicting emotions and didn't linger on either feeling.

He didn't respond to the text. He had two calls to make. Chief Hull wouldn't be surprised by another contact.

When he next saw Dale, Phil hoped his partner would understand the value of the second.

~~~

Goodman was snoring by the time I reached the quagmire where 235, 35, and 80 intersect. Probably an innate talent refined over years of late-night stake outs with Phil, if that was something police officers still did.

Catching I-80 West, the sounds of ethereal folk music merged with a view to the end of the world, horizontal sky meeting acre after acre of flat-iron fields, round one-ton hay bales, and the residue of an early corn harvest. In other times I barely noticed the miles of familiar landscape: livestock, free-range dogs, the occasional quarter horse, farms extending from massive corporate intrusions to tidy, upscale family acreages to lean, downtrodden holdouts. Today, the sight of even the most careworn homesteads was tame alongside the reality of Carlos Musslewhite's farmhouse death.

When will we catch up with Phil? Where's Seth? What if we don't catch up with Phil? What if we get to the Nebraska border and haven't found anybody? What's going on with Dad?

The tempo of the band accompanied my racing thoughts. I nudged the game of rotating unanswerable questions to the back of my brain and concentrated on keeping the car between the lines, speeding toward a purple disappearing into black horizon. I blew by the Highway 71 South exit to Villisca, the site of the 1912 unsolved axe murders, the gruesome slaughter of eight people as they slept. I shuddered every time I passed through what naïve east coast novelists would describe as "a sleepy village where nothing ever happens."

Musslewhite. Villisca. More than a century apart.

The phone pinged on the console, rousing Goodman. He poked the screen and read the message.

"It's the lieutenant. We're going to the police station in Avoca." He slapped the dashboard, a rare show of enthusiasm. "They found Seth."

My accelerator foot shook.

"Alive?"

"Alive."

I slowed to 55, letting traffic pass by until I was steady on the wheel. "Where's Phil?"

"All I know is that Avoca PD and their on-call doc have cleared Seth's release to you and me. Take the exit to 59."

He knew we would come.

"I know the way."

Restored to a manageable rush of energy, I challenged the speed limit for the last twenty miles before rounding the curve onto 59 South. Goodman calmed himself by hijacking the last of the root beer. A batch of pheasants were sightseeing from the shoulder, ignorant to the perils of careless drivers and the approach of hunting season. We passed a well-kept, nondescript motel on the northern outskirts of town. The parking lot was jammed with law enforcement vehicles. A fair share of the local citizenry had gathered to observe and get the rumor mill in motion.

Go home people. It was one call from a scared kid.

The roads in rural Iowa often become named streets, returning to numbers again on the far side. Highway 59 became North Chestnut. The police department was a couple of blocks off the main drag. I knew this because J.R. had once sent me to Atlantic with a trunk load of concentrated root beer syrup for a restaurant owner buddy. Clocking through Avoca at forty-five in a twenty-five zone in a well-used Buick full of glass jugs that looked like an illegal liquid substance earned me a trip to the Avoca PD. Dad vouched for me, confirming the dense brown contents as root beer, not moonshine or toxic waste. I escaped with a warning.

Old memories collided with current realities when I pulled into a fifteen-minute parking space and shut the car down. Goodman lifted the bag of remaining chicken and potato salad. "A snack for local law enforcement. Professional courtesy." He groaned his heft out of the car. "Wait here."

"Not a chance."

He slammed the door as an answer and trudged alone down a wide concrete walkway toward the dim lobby of the public services building. I put my hand on the door latch.

Wrong time for a power struggle, Anderson.

I sat back and stretched into the low-grade ache throughout my body, my eyes riveted on the entrance, time slowing to a crawl as it does when need is urgent.

Thankfully, our pilgrim's face shined through the twilight in less time than mandated by the street sign, his walk slow and careful. Goodman aimed him toward the back door of the car and redeposited himself in the front passenger seat.

"Seth. Good to see you."

"Mr. Anderson. " Seth smiled lazily between sips of bottled water. "Likewise."

Although his spare physique was lost somewhere in a loaned Avoca Vikings sweatshirt, this was a different young man than the one I met in my office. His voice had lost much of its frailty. A 40W light in his eyes had replaced the look of complete bewilderment.

I had a catch in my throat.

From worry to joy.

I contained the strength of my emotion. "How you feeling?"

"Still tired and weak. But the pancakes and coffee the nice woman from the diner dropped off were delicious.

Talking to Mom and Dad helped..." His cheerfulness did a sudden descent into a cascade of tears, his breath coming in gulps, his slight chest heaving up and out.

The drugs are active, but wearing off. Lifting the cap off his trauma.

I rested my hand on the seat back. He grasped it, his strength waning as he released a dose of pent-up fear. We sat until his breath regulated. Goodman handed him a bleached white linen handkerchief. Clutching the hanky, he set his water in the cup holder, and mastered the seatbelt. Curling into the corner, he closed his eyes, and, within moments, sank into a wheezing sleep.

"Damn. I wish I could sleep like that."

"Not if you had to go through what he's been through to get there. Where's Phil?"

Goodman's ringtone—*Birdland* by Weather Report—interrupted. Instead of answering me, he answered the phone.

"Hey. What's up?"

Phil.

"How'd you find them?"

Find who?

"You did. Why?"

Goodman's annoyed.

"Yeah. We have him. Sleeping. He's in pretty good shape considering." He hesitated. "One thing and it's not a request."

It was unlike Goodman to make demands on Phil.

"Don't do anything heroic before we get to you and gum up the story I'm gonna tell back in Des Moines about how I saved your butt." I felt his eyes shift to me. "Sure. Phil wants to talk to you."

He handed me the phone.

"Make it quick, I'm driving." I was more than annoyed.

"I remember asking you to stay put," he started.

"I remember your sermons about caution and teamwork, too," I shot back. "Catherine came to the office and asked for my help. You scared the hell out of her."

"Yes, I was wrong," he admitted. "I spoke with her. She was relieved and told me we'd discuss this further when I get home."

"Goodman asked me to ride along."

"Oh." The starch went out of his lecture.

"Where are you?"

"Good news."

The man's an expert at diversion.

"Where are you?"

"I'm on my way to the Lake Manawa exit," he said. "The State Patrol found the rest of the kids in a truck stop restaurant."

His tone was overly composed, even for Phil.

"That's wonderful." A new alarm bell went off in my head before I had time to feel the relief. "What's the bad news."

"The state troopers have surrounded a white van in the parking lot. There's someone in the driver's seat, but they can't see who through the tinted glass. They aren't getting a response."

I heard a voice in the background.

"I need to go. Dale will fill you in. We'll talk when you get here."

Cell phones go silent when people hang up on you. I tossed the phone on the dashboard.

"Wind it up and keep going west," Goodman ordered.

I turned the engine over and U-turned, retracing our route to the interstate and fast-tracking us toward Council Bluffs. Goodman talked, validating my guess that our passenger had been drugged, but catching me completely off-guard with his report that Emma was one of the villains.

"According to the kids, Braxton drove them to the truck stop. They met Emma, who must have beat tracks to Manawa after Seth got away from her in Avoca. She sent the group inside for a meal and that's the last the students saw of them. Like Phil said, somebody is sitting in the driver's seat."

He gave me a few seconds to catch up.

"One of them could be hiding out of sight," I said. "What happens next?"

Goodman explained, making sure to include all of the ways things could go haywire.

It was one of the rare times I was sorry I'd asked another question.

~~~

Braxton had followed the plan. He stopped outside of Avoca and dialed Emma. Who didn't pick up. He gave it a few minutes, then bailed on her half-baked orders and cruised the motel.

No truck. No SUV.

He took a calculated risk and parked down the block, hidden on the far side of a used car lot. He checked his human cargo. Not comatose, but out for the count.

He'd changed clothes before leaving the farm. He strolled onto a back street, a local guy in a John Deere ballcap, gray sweat shirt, and jeans. Several blocks south, he approached the motor lodge like he belonged there. He knocked softly on the door of Room 23.

No voices. No answer.

He knocked a second time.

Nothing.

He turned in time to see the motel manager walk into the parking lot. Braxton stepped behind an outdoor drink machine before he was spotted and they both watched the sky beyond the tree line fill with flashing lights, red, white, and blue, reflected through the dusk. He didn't need to hear sirens to know who the lights belonged to or where they were headed. He ducked around the north corner of the motel and sprinted for the van, the grind of vehicles braking hard on gravel reverberating over his shoulder.

There was a minimum of movement in the back when he put the van in gear. Keeping to the speed limit, he crossed the bridge over the interstate, eyes open for back roads to buy himself time. Choosing random turns, his fear gradually converted to ten miles of anger, raging through him like a vintage pinball machine on the edge of tilt.

No Seth. No Emma. Cops everywhere. Here he was, left with a load of stupefied rich kids passed out in a rickety-assed van, rolling down two-lane country roads, hoping he could avoid the APB that had, without a doubt, been heard by every hick in the state with a badge and a gun.

It wasn't like running was new. He'd spent a lifetime dodging the authorities. Hell, he was born in Mitchellville. The women's prison, not the town. Mom hadn't exactly followed the straight and narrow path.

Taranis found him in Denver. Found the whole crew. Gave them a safe place to live. Food. Became their teacher. Picking pockets. Shoplifting. Rolling drunks. Setting up perps who thought they were going to a no-tell motel and, instead, gave up cash and credit card number to keep their families from hearing about their twisted recreational activities. Hit quick and move on to another city before they got noticed by the cops.

It was a good gig, until he and Musslewhite got tired of taking the biggest chances, while Taranis took the biggest cut. When they left, he told them they'd get clipped. He was right.

He found them again. Doing time on parole, backbreaking day labor in the aftermath of the forest fires. One more time they disappeared into the void of missing souls.

The new deal had been a grand slam. Get off the streets and target college students, lonely kids with discretionary income, willing to pay dues for a social life with the window dressing Taranis pitched as a deep spiritual connection. Card numbers, PINS, ATM withdrawals. The crew embedded themselves in the groups, encouraging the marks to continue in their pursuit of universal truth when they moved on to spread the word, pulling from their endless list of identities to reboot the game in another town.

But, Taranis wanted more. He told them the gig was "a mere stepping stone." He had the payoff to end all payoffs.

Braxton figured he'd escaped Iowa forever. But, the whole isolation in rural Iowa thing had been his idea. He's been shipped all over the state as a kid. He knew the terrain, understood how to find an abandoned property, and how to keep a low profile in places where a stranger stood out like a foreigner.

Taranis and Emma did the rest, handpicking a batch of wealthy students hungry for friends and adventure. Get them to the farm. No phone service. No internet. The crew on the inside. Isolation and control.

Perfect. Until Emma and Carlos went over the deep end.

"So the kid has bad dreams. Who doesn't?" Braxton had gone off on his partners in the garden shed. But he was outvoted. Musslewhite would take Seth into town and get something to calm the guy's head until they could finish the deal, Emma claiming to be an expert on that sort of thing.

Now Carlos, his only friend, had ODed. Taranis had stopped all communication. Emma was trying to take over the operation. And he was on the run with the excess baggage.

Something didn't fit.

Lost in his tirade, he missed the sign —the arrow for Sharp Curve. He hit the bend in the road at 60 mph, dropping onto the shoulder. The tires fought to grip loose stone. He over-compensated to the left and the top-heavy ride threatened to roll. An instinct for self-preservation yanked his foot off the pedal. The engine stalled and the van's momentum rolled them to the edge of a drainage ditch.

His heart thundered into his throat.

"Killing us isn't the new plan, Kenton," he muttered to himself.

He looked over his shoulder. It was mind-boggling. Strapped in, the kids were still lights out. The extra stash packed a punch. Coaxing the van back to life, his hands were shaking when the burner vibrated. He palmed it from his pocket.

"Where are you?" His rasp masked the near-death moment.

"Shut up!" Emma's new favorite phrase. "Get to Lake Manawa. Truck parking at the first stop north of the highway." She hung up before he got another word out.

He slammed the phone against the dashboard, cracking the screen. A single member of his payload finally startled back to semi-consciousness. "Sorry, Sister. My hand slipped. It was Sister Emma. She drove on ahead. We're going to meet her up the road for a good night's sleep."

The students had been too disoriented to question the absence of Emma, or the man they called Lawrence. At the mention of her name and the prospects of an end to the road trip, though, Contessa eked out, "Thank you, Brother," and slumped back into the seat.

A mile north of the interstate, self-preservation supplanted Braxton's anger and he made his decision. There was no way he could keep his passengers under wraps for much longer. It was time to lighten his load. He needed to find out if Emma had Seth under control, grab as much more of the money as he could get his hands on, and book it for parts unknown. His best exit strategy was the one that didn't lead back to prison.

He slowed and turned into a lot jammed with semis, an area drivers used to sleep before beating the traffic, and maybe the state patrol, on an all-night ride. Rounding the grid of trucks, engines on idle, he spotted the black SUV hidden among the tractor-trailers, camouflaged with mud splatters, dents, and new plates. He couldn't see anyone through the tinted glass.

Emma was out of the vehicle by the time he turned off his headlights and coasted into the shadows. He confirmed the heft of the pistol he kept under the driver's seat before she slammed open the sliding back door. Insurance.

One by one, the kids reacted to the noise, opening their eyes into a mix of drugs and disorientation.

"So happy to see you, friends." Emma's counterfeit effervescence was on high octane. She'd traded in her flimsy peasant garb for form fitting jeans, her long, straight hair tucked into a blue-on-gray Iowa Western Community College hoodie. "And you, too, Brother."

"Missed you Sister," he lied in return.

"Time for a feast and a comfortable bed, campers," she said, pointing toward the truck stop. "Head into the restaurant. Brother Theodore and I will be in shortly. We'll all eat to our heart's delight."

Feast? Braxton centered on the word apoplectic, from a highbrow book Taranis had given him years ago. The definition fit with his impulse to put his hands around Emma's throat and squeeze.

He controlled his urge for violence and mimicked her cheerful tone. "Yes. We'll order everything on the menu, campers."

Bolstered by the prospect of a hot meal, the students struggled out of their seatbelts. The group stumbled from the van and, arms linked, zigzagged across the pavement into the eatery.

With the whole gang inside, Emma pulled the hood over her head and slithered in through the passenger door.

Braxton fought to hold his surface calm.

"Why weren't you at the motel? Where's Oberstreet?"

His shock lagged one unfortunate click behind his confrontation. Emma forced a 9mm from the left side of the hoodie's kangaroo pocket. The suppressor she'd attached caught on the fold, throwing off her close quarters aim. Her first shot blew a hole in his extended right hand. The bullet passed through, grazed his shoulder and buried blood and skin into the seat cushion, damage enough to dull his reaction time. He clawed under the seat, screams filling the van until, pinned by the pounding of bullets invading his body, he came to rest.

~~~

Phil squeezed into the loaner vest supplied by a trooper with the frame of a body builder, his eyes riveted on the van holding one or more fugitives. He rested a hand over his hip holster, his relaxed outer shell at war with the desire to pull his weapon and charge the vehicle.

"You'll stand down on this, Detective."

Phil was positioned behind a squad car, next to Major Sunderman, the formidable looking commander whose brown-on-tan jacket, Kevlar vest, and campaign hat gave her a distinct military bearing.

"My tactical team has it from here," she said. She'd read through his mask.

A dozen androgynous troopers in black uniforms, face masks, helmets and vests had formed a perimeter around the van at the north end of the truck stop, weapons trained on the silhouette in the driver's seat. As soon as the Iowa State Patrol hit the parking lot, all exits had been closed off. Road officers moved from semi to semi, escorting the surprised truckers behind a brick storage building at the east end of the lot. Additional troopers were parked crosswise at the entrances, directing travelers back onto the interstate.

The crisis negotiator had listed all options over the bullhorn. In truth, there was only one—lose your weapons and give yourselves up. Now.

There was no reaction from the van. A lone figure remained barely visible, behind aftermarket darkened windows.

The major nodded. The lieutenant spoke into a headset and organized hell busted loose. The circle of officers power walked forward. Glass shattered. A flash grenade detonated. The interior of the van was flooded with blinding light and a deafening bang. In concert, front and back doors sprung open. No shots were fired.

Within seconds, distant highway sounds returned to replace the flash and bang.

"All clear. All clear. All clear," floated through the smoke.

The lieutenant, gun trained on the driver, pulled the photos provided by Phil from beneath his body armor. Phil saw him touch his radio.

Major Sunderman took her headset off.

"Only one, Detective. We'll need your help for an ID."

~~~

The hum in Emma's ears confirmed that silencers were not silent. Especially in a closed space, coupled with penetrating screams.

She shuddered, swallowed hard to clear her hearing, and forced herself to stretch past her former ally to shut off the van. She reached under the driver's seat for whatever he had frantically lunged for. Another hand gun, lighter, smaller, and shinier than her spent weapon. She didn't know much about firearms and didn't care, as long as a bullet came out if she needed to pull the trigger.

Under her seat was his cut of the cash.

She didn't wait to find out if anyone heard Braxton die. Money bag over her shoulder, she lowered her head and willed herself to walk back to the idling SUV at an easy pace, guns against both legs, barrels toward the ground. Dots of his blood shined across her hoodie when the dome light blinked on. She slid his gun under the seat, pealed the hoodie off, and tossed it on the passenger floor mat with her weapon. Grabbing a clean fleece from her bag, she tucked her hair under a University of Nebraska Cornhuskers cap and checked the dashboard clock.

An hour to make it to Eppley Airport.

She drove away from the lake, avoiding I-29 on the Iowa side of the Missouri River. It was easy to find a desolate turnoff. She wrapped her gun in the bloodstained hoodie and pitched them in the river. Settling back in the SUV, obeying every traffic law, she conjured up one of Taranis' favorite maxims in an effort to erase the final snapshot of Braxton in her head.

Plan, then adapt.

He'd told her this was their superpower. "There's no diploma, kid. You have street smarts and you're forward thinking. The guys are good soldiers, but true leaders are creative and daring. That's our gift, yours and mine."

It had taken time to discover what no one, not even Taranis, understood. She had powers beyond street smarts, talents even he lacked. Her ability to feign genuine interest and light up a room with her smile came without effort. With practice, she learned how to use her energy to distract, entice, and, more recently, gain the trust of pampered rich kids. She channeled her hate into the dance.

A lack of remorse or empathy—the headline on the evaluation from one of the list of places they'd bounced in and out of before Taranis found them in a booth in the mom-and-pop diner outside of Boulder, ready to skip the ticket. Runaways, they'd been two days without a meal. He paid the tab and took them in.

Lucky for them, Taranis was interested in using kids to commit crimes, not committing crimes against kids. They hit every state from North Dakota to New Mexico. She smiled at the memory of her first taste of guacamole in Santa Fe. Life was good until Musslewhite and Braxton left and got busted. Better when they returned and Taranis gave them all the blueprint for the big score.

It was a good blueprint. But, hers was better.

Her insides seethed.

Things were going to plan when she convinced Musslewhite to expel Levi. The rest of the group became even more timid. Then, Carlos pushed Seth too far.

It wasn't her fault they'd sent him to the wrong kind of shrink. Filing through her childhood, prescribing drugs while they hammered on her to stay off drugs. She thought they all gave pills to straighten your head out. It was Musslewhite who thought Anderson sounded like a soft touch in the online article about a B&E at his house. Another of his screw-ups.

Once they were exposed, anticipating a visit from the heat had been a no-brainer. But sending Seth to the creek to hide, with no one to keep an eye on him, had been one bad decision too far. When Carlos sent Braxton back to find the boy, he was gone. Lost in the woods. Musslewhite had become a liability.

They caught a break when the tracker on the pickup kicked in. It had to be Seth. He'd found his way back to the farm, coherent enough to go on the run. Finding the low rent motel had been easy. But, after she ditched the truck, the room was empty. How could she have known the spacey egghead was some kind of escape artist?

Without Seth under wraps, she needed to cut their losses.

In all their years of working the streets, she had never killed anyone. Now, two dead in one week.

His text interrupted her ruminations.

"I'm here."

Maybe three.

Emma pulled the Cornhuskers cap tight above her plain glass tortoise shell frames and placed the fake rideshare sign in the windshield. Saying a pirate's prayer for the Wyoming plates they'd stolen, she pulled out of the cell phone lot onto Abbot Drive. It was easy to follow the signs for passenger pick-up. She drove aggressively enough to look like she belonged. A thin, unmemorable twenty-something stood with his army green backpack at the pick-up spot. She pulled to the curb. He stepped from under the lights, opened the door, and dropped into the seat next to her. In less than ten seconds, they blended into the flow of traffic, passing two airport cops without notice.

Medium brown oilskin jacket, pony-tail trailing behind a camo ball cap. The label on the box of hair dye had read Light Brown. He'd replaced his rimless glasses with black frames as soon as he left camp.

"Did you get it?" From her peripheral vision, she saw him pat the backpack. "Is he dead?"

"Yes and no. I don't know," he said. "I almost didn't make it from the bus station. There was a snow storm in the mountains. A bad one. I barely made it in and out of there. I hit him and grabbed everything I could carry." He overexplained when he thought he was in trouble. "I had to get back to the airport and get rid of the truck."

"What the hell does yes and no mean?" She kept herself from shouting, knowing he'd withdraw into himself.

"I can't get through Seth's new walls." The account numbers and layers of security they'd pieced together from Oberstreet had been altered.

He shrunk into the seat, talking fast. "But I got everything we need to find the money Taranis hid in other places." He pulled a USB drive from his coat pocket. "I'm working on the transfer to our accounts."

If the answer had come from anyone else, Emma would have stopped and hammered his face to a pulp. But this man was special. Their former boss had encouraged his passion for IT, using his genius to hack credit card accounts and redirect deliveries of everything from smart TVs to pizzas at dummy drop sites monitored by the crew. He'd even set up a dummy website with dead end contact information for the student conference.

More important, he was the only person she had ever loved. The person she was bound to protect.

She let some of the air out of her temper and merged onto the main drag.

"Well, that's something."

"I feel kind of bad," he said. "Taranis got us off the streets."

"Which is where we land without additional resources. Or would it have been better to hang around for the police to figure out who we are and let him ride off into the sunset with enough money to set himself up with a new crew?"

"No." He hung his head like he did every time she argued him into a corner.

She aimed toward the city, already absorbed in mapping out another set of moves. "Let's find a safe place to spend the night. We'll get something to eat and see what can be salvaged from what you boys screwed up."

Division of labor. He was tech. She was logistics.

"Good idea." He smiled, pushing his glasses up the bridge of his nose with a forefinger. "Missed you, Sis."

"Missed you more, Bro." She playfully punched him in the arm. "Emma to you, Levi."

No one but themselves knew their real names. No one but themselves and Taranis had known they were sister and brother.

~~~

Phil held his badge at eye level and approached the van. The smoke had been swept away by a steady wind, revealing another grisly death. The former Kenton Braxton, his sweat shirt a tie-dye pattern of deep red, blackened holes in the centers. The second member of The Scholars of Calm murdered in as many days. It was a demoralizing way to prove his theory. Emma was a killer. Who remained one step ahead of him.

"Snap out of it, Anderson." Goodman realized he'd lost me in his barrage of possible outcomes if the highway patrol took the van by force. "There's a whole bunch of kids who might need you in a few minutes."

"*What bunch of kids?*" Seth's drowsy question rose over the seat.

"We found your pals, safe and sound," Goodman said.

"That's amazing!"

Another measure of peace passed through me to see a living, breathing Seth in the mirror.

"How you doing, young fellow?" Goodman sounded like he cared.

"Every time I wake up, I feel a little stronger, Detective. It's like my brain is rebooting." He took a swig of water. "Which reminds me, where are we going?"

I pointed into the distance at a beacon of USA flag neon lighting up the twilight. "Your friends are inside that truck stop."

"Wonderful!" He went back to serious. "I do have one more question. Is somebody going to explain to me exactly what's been going on?"

"Soon. First, let's check in with your buddies and get you something to eat."

"Sounds good."

Seth's anticipation filled the car as we rounded the exit ramp. Two state troopers gave us the universal palm forward signal to halt at the truck stop entrance. Goodman lowered the window and flashed his badge.

"Detective Goodman from Des Moines." He pointed a thumb toward Seth. "This is another one of the students, part of the group your people sequestered in the restaurant. The driver is Hank Anderson, his therapist. We're here to connect up with Detective Evans. I was told to ask for Major Sunderman."

The guy didn't take our word for any of it. "Goodman. Huh. Stay put, men." He lowered his jaw and spoke into his mic while his partner gave us the once over with a flashlight big enough to beat us to death. My gut butterfly reacted.

We're all on the same side here, Anderson. Take it easy.

The first officer tapped the roof. "You'll find them at the main entrance. Park on the south side of the building." He waved us on.

I eased through a pack of law enforcement vehicles and several box-shaped ambulances crowding the building. Bypassing a cluster of curious truckers in shirt sleeves and insulated vests, I stopped on the dark side of the gaudy neon. I slipped into a hoodie and Goodman handed Seth a nylon jacket big enough for a couple of guys his size. Around the corner, nightfall was held at bay by the synthetic daylight of the parking lot. An open-air tent had been erected to the right of the entrance into the building, surrounded by uniformed highway officers. The harsh standing work lights and Phil's height made him an easy find in the crowded command center. In close quarters, with a wrinkled shirt and loosened tie, he was more rumpled than I had ever seen him. He was hatless, holding his fedora in deference to a senior officer.

"Your call, Detective." The gold oak leaves on the shoulders of the officer's uniform identified her as the person of authority. "First, let's meet these people."

"Major Sunderman, this is my partner, Detective Goodman. And our colleague, Hank Anderson."

I was sure I saw Goodman sneer at the sergeant standing off the major's left shoulder. The trooper seemed to look right through him.

"This must be the young man I've been wanting to meet." There was a tenderness in Phil's tone I knew was typically saved for his wife and children. "Seth Oberstreet, I presume."

"Yes, sir. You must be Detective Evans. I recognize your voice. Chief Hull from Avoca said I needed to thank you again for coming to help me." Seth looked past Phil, spotted his fellow camp members through the glass circling the truck stop dining room, and lost his footing. Phil took his shoulders and steadied him.

"Your friends are safe."

Seth melted, staggering into the big man. Throwing his arms around as much of the detective as he could reach, he buried his head into Phil's herculean chest. Stoicism be damned, Phil hugged him back. He stared into the dark. I guessed he was in prayer, or picturing Matthew, or both.

"I have one request for you, Mr. Oberstreet." The major pressed on.

Seth stood back and wiped his face with the sleeve of Goodman's jacket.

"Just Seth." He took in the oak leaves on her uniform. "Major."

"Seth, it would be useful if you could give my sergeant descriptions of Emma and Levi, who are the individuals still missing from your group."

Empower him by giving him a job.

"Yes, ma'am. I mean Major." Seth's slip of tongue brought a blush to his cheeks.

"Not a problem." Her eyes reviewed the scene. "Ma'am is much nicer than some of the names I'm called."

Seth's shoulders relaxed. She'd put him at ease in a sixty-second exchange.

Impressive.

Major Sunderman motioned to her officer. With a better view, I noticed his name badge said Goodman. He was familiar from the neck up, but, in dad's words, built like he was made out of pipe cleaners, the opposite of our

Goodman's stout frame. I decided to rein in my curiosity for the time being.

"Come with me, young man. Let's check in with your friends."

Phil, composure reinstalled, gave Seth a pat on the back to confirm our lost-and-found student was steady enough to be escorted inside. By the time they parted the sliding doors, Seth had engaged the sergeant in a loose account of his escape, interspersed with visual sketches of the crooks at-large.

"Hank." Phil called me into the circle, an outsider invited to an insiders' confab. "The Major set up an assist from the BCI. Their forensic team is at the van." He turned to his partner. "Dale, we've been instructed by the department to assist the Major and her team." Goodman's face sagged in relief. They still had jobs. "Since you're up to speed on these people, would you head over and provide support from our end." Phil nodded toward the semis at rest. "It's Braxton and it's ugly."

"Will do." Goodman resumed the cadence of their years together. Apparently, their near miss at career demolition was already old news.

"Mr. Anderson." The major addressed me in formal tones, intruding on my shock that another bad guy was dead. "You're the mental health professional. I need someone to assess the mental status of these young people. The medical team has cleared the restaurant of stray travelers and set up a triage center. The manager graciously agreed to close the site to customers for now. We pressed a few truckers—ex-military folks—into service. Two physicians and a nurse practitioner are on the way. Can you provide us with an opportunity to cover all the bases?"

Phil eyeballed me, knowing I'd be tempted to salute.

Decorum, Anderson.

"Happy to help, Major."

"Detective Evans and I will coordinate contact with the families and the search for the SUV driven by the individual known to us as Emma. Based on reports from several students who confirm she was present when they left the van, we believe Emma killed Kenton Braxton." She rubbed her hands as if warming to the task at hand. "If there are no questions, let's get to it."

Musslewhite and Braxton were dead. Emma was a killer on the loose. I had a bunch of questions, but didn't want to disrupt my fragile membership on the team. I did catch Goodman's eye before he walked away.

"Sergeant Goodman?"

"Like I said, Anderson. Family business." He looked like he'd taken a swig of sour milk. "You'll like each other. He's the one who sticks his nose into everybody's business." He stomped away.

Before heading out to my appointed rounds, I also wagged a finger at Phil, instructing him to lean down to my level. "You, of course, let your wife know you still have a job." I tried to give him my best version of stern.

"I did." He tried to look repentant, assuming a more authentic glare in no time. "Who does not remember directing you to go on the road with Dale. You will both be hearing from her."

I spun on my heels and headed for the door. "Looking forward to it."

"In the meantime," Phil grumbled at my back. "She says thank you."

Given a pass by the officer inside the door, I ignored the ping of the first text message in my pants pocket. By the time I reached my assigned area, it repeated four more times. I stopped.

Belinda. Dennis. Belinda. Dennis. Jill.

Countermanding my generally accepted Hank Anderson anti-technological policy, I texted the duo.

All of us are safe. Stop. I'm in Lake Manawa. Stop. Please let Gail know. Love to all. Stop. If tempted to text again, stop.

Having the good sense not to ask Belinda to update Jill, I sent her a similar message. Forgoing the smart-aleck telegraph reference, I substituted a smiling sun emoji, then jammed the phone back into my pocket before anybody could ignore my instructions and respond.

Smile emoji? Not your fault, Anderson. It's been a rough day.

Inside I found a bustling impromptu care center, lights muted, staffed by paramedics, EMTs, and a rugged pack of truckers moonlighting as lift-and-carry personnel. Several more serious looking troopers surveyed the proceedings. A cadre of waitstaff and night cooks had rearranged the cherry red vinyl booths into a line of temporary beds. They'd set the Formica tables end to end and brought forth a collection of sights and smells reminiscent of a hometown church potluck—a full array of menu items neatly displayed in line with ceramic plates, silverware, urns of coffee and ice water, various juices, and soda. Empty cups and dishes were strewn throughout the café turned mobile ER.

I scanned the room for Seth, who was stretched out among the grouping of students reclined in booths, pillows under heads, covered by blankets gathered from surrounding vehicles. Most of the patients, including my guy, were asleep, several connected to IVs. I counted two students awake but not alert. The medical team quietly and methodically circulated, checking machines, making notes, speaking softly. A long folding table was positioned against the wall, packed with laptop computers and medical supplies, known and unknown to me. A wiry man with a serious tan, shaved head, and trim auburn beard, the sleeves of a black ambulance service pullover pushed up his forearms, peeled off a pair of baby blue surgical gloves and waved me over.

"You must be the therapist Major Sunderman told me would check on the kids. I'm the team supervisor." He motioned as if introducing the room. "The young man you transported hugged his pals, ate a quick bite, and hit the sack. Most of our patients have eaten and had plenty to drink. Vital signs have been checked. Some are dehydrated and we're working on that."

He stopped to watch one fellow attempt to stand, waver, and sink back into a chair, staring at his legs as if clueless about the betrayal of his body. A rangy caramel-skinned woman in the same uniform as my contact sat next to the kid and mouthed, "I've got this."

"I think that's your first customer, Mr. Anderson."

"It's Hank."

"Trevor." He shook my hand. "We're pretty sure someone has been doping them, but no one presents life-threatening withdrawal symptoms, Hank. It appears they were all dosed enough to keep them malleable." His anger burned through an air of calm. "By somebody who knew what they were doing."

Lawrence. Knew what he was doing. Until he didn't.

"We don't have enough transport vehicles and no one is in urgent distress, so we set ourselves up to monitor them here," he explained. "Cass, Page, and Mills Counties are sending ambulances for more rides. The restaurant people have been great. We're in constant communication with one of the ER docs, who's on the way."

"How about I talk with the two who are awake. I'll check in with you after the assessments."

"Sounds good."

"How's the coffee."

"Top shelf."

A fellow connoisseur.

"Have a bite to eat," he said. "You look a little worse for wear yourself."

The mention of food gave me a small rush of energy.

"Make sure to keep that wound on your chin clean, too," he noted. "Shaving accident?"

"Falling off bicycle onto my face accident."

He snapped a clean set of gloves onto his hands and shook his head like a man who thought he'd seen it all. "Bicycle accidents. Multi-car wrecks. ODs. Gunshot wounds. I've never been called out on anything like the one we've got here tonight."

He escorted and introduced me to my first patient, who turned out to be Marcel, the owner of the phone Seth took with him when he left the farm. Brief mental status exams of Marcel and his friend, Contessa, yielded similar results. Both were verbal, knew their names and addresses, had no idea of the date, and were baffled by the circumstances that landed them in an Iowa truck stop on a cloudy autumn night. In monotones, free of facial affect, each offered disjointed stories of their journey from college student to unknowing captives of The Scholars of Calm.

Like my first session with Seth.

They were eager to go home. Neither expressed the idea or intention of harming themselves or anyone else. Despite exhaustion and sedation, both fought to remain awake, fearful that someone from The Scholars would return. I rotated, offering assurances of safety to them and four more students who startled awake, listening to early attempts to process the walking nightmare they'd all experienced. Within each interaction, dog-tired watchfulness was eventually superseded by my promise that no one from The Scholars could penetrate the state patrol's security. One-by-one they fell into a sound sleep.

I waved at the head paramedic and tipped my head toward a private corner. "For now, everybody I sat with is understandably anxious, confused, and relatively stable."

"Perhaps most important, asleep." he said. "For now?"

"As these folks detox and reconnect with the outside world, a whole range of after-effects could surface, impacted by pre-existing mental health and addiction concerns, health histories, level of resilience and vulnerability, level of family support, past trauma history."

"Along with other individualized factors." He finished my sentence for me, typing my report with one hand, onto a tablet.

"Exactly."

"Recommendations?" He was already in what's next mode.

"Keep them stable. Let them sleep. If anyone wakes up from a nightmare, or just wants to talk, grab me. Get them to a hospital for observation as soon as possible. Have each of them re-assessed by trauma specialists."

I went through my internal check list. "Make sure the social work staff coordinates follow-up care. These people are from all over the country. Their families may not be aware of the risks and the resources available in their home communities."

Trevor added to his notes, then tucked his pad under an arm. "Thanks. By the way, I've heard about you."

"Me?"

"Emergency care is a small world. Jeff and I went to school together."

"Jeff, our friendly neighborhood Des Moines EMT?" I'd been on the receiving end of Jeff's services via 911 calls twice during the first mess in the fall.

"The same. He thinks you're a pretty kick-ass guy."

"More like got-my-ass-kicked guy."

He lightly elbowed me. "Jeff said you were funny."

Trevor reminded me of his instructions to eat and drink. As my world tends to turn, a life-affirming bottle of A&W root beer led to leftover meatloaf packed with onions and green peppers, a side of garlic mashed potatoes, finished off with a fist-sized caramel roll, kept fragrant and soft in a stainless-steel warming tray. I exchanged pleasantries with an athletic, sunbaked trucker whose jean jacket announced her as Mabel in large bedazzled letters stitched on the back. Her cap said, U.S. Marine Corps, Retired.

"You're a cute little guy. I could just put you in my pocket and take you home." She handed me a fresh cup of coffee.

I only had a low wattage grin left in me. "I'm afraid you might break me in half, Mabel."

She winked before lifting a case of waters to distribute to her comrades. "You'd expire with a smile on your face, young fellow."

I chewed on that thought, and a second roll.

As personnel from the outlying counties trickled in, I was directed to an empty booth, where I could rest, in the event there was an additional need for my services. I wrapped myself in the blanket and sat upright, to remain vigilant.

It worked until I fell asleep.

~~~

The siblings had stopped for drinks and snacks on the way to finding a motel on the outer edges of civilization. It wouldn't be their first.

The bored kid behind the counter was locked in on the hard-scrabble woman on his iPad screen. Mabel, a long-distance trucker, was having her minute in the spotlight on a late Breaking News report about a remarkable situation in Council Bluffs. She told the camera that a group of students were being cared for at a makeshift ER within a truck stop and would be transported the next morning to a local hospital.

"There's a real dandy little counselor type who helped free a bunch of college kids held against their will by a group of godless radicals at a camp somewhere in Polk County," she said. "A bunch of my fellow truckers are providing back up until they could be evaced to the closest medical facility." The reporter gave the name of a hospital on the Nebraska side of the Missouri River, a short ride into Omaha.

Levi thought it was a fluke they'd stopped at the convenience store.

Emma thought the universe had sent them a sign. One more chance to hit the jackpot.

SATURDAY

Taranis opened his eyes to a feeble attempt at dawn creeping through the steady curtain of snow, a swirling threat of whiteout on the backside of the ice storm.

His lingering hangover was a pinprick in comparison to the sensation that a hard object had tried to bury itself in his skull. He remained still and kept his breath shallow. Straining beyond the pain and leftover booze, he listened for sounds of the attacker he'd so clumsily allowed to ambush him.

There was nothing but the undertone of a hammering wind against the high-impact windows.

He rolled onto his stomach and staggered to his feet, suppressing waves of nausea. Settling in a stance wide enough to anchor himself, he stepped around the walking stick that usually leaned outside the back door, absent the crust of blood coating the knob at the thick end.

There was an empty space on the kitchen table where the laptop had waited for the magic numbers. He felt the pocket of his pants. The burner phone was gone, too.

He knew who his visitor had been. Smart. Quiet. Lock skills. Too scared to finish the job.

How had they learned of this place?

The answer magnified his pain. Make sure the mark doesn't know you're listening and watching. A message he drilled into them, year after year. A stray receipt? A phone hack while he slept? Somehow, he had failed to follow his own edict.

His nausea exploded and painted the table with the remains of last night's dinner.

Collapsing into a hardwood chair, he touched the wet, pulsating lump behind his temple. Warm blood trickled down his neck, giving rise to a loathing so powerful it erased his awareness of the bitter temperatures closing in on his lost hideaway. He struggled to his feet and went in search of the bottle. It held just enough for medicinal purposes. Pouring himself two inches straight up, he gulped and weaved his way to the study.

The wall safe was open. Empty. USB drive. Back-up burners. Account numbers. Passwords. Gone. His protege would break through his encryption in no time and move things out of reach, cloud or no cloud.

The crystal tumbler shattered, drops of amber liquid dripping from the exposed timber. He stared at his empty hand, willing himself back to restraint. He lowered into the softness of his cushioned rocker, emptying his mind until the impulse to destroy everything in sight retreated to a distant corner of his damaged core. Straightening his spine, he closed his eyes and connected with the gift that had freed him from the streets.

He planned.

Mentor. Protector. He rescued all of them. He knew them better than they knew themselves. Where they had been. Where they would go. Who they would become to get there.

He did not think of himself as a violent man. He was an artist, not a thug. It was true he'd hurt some people. Never out of anger or malice. Only in service of the job.

This was different.

Standing too quickly, the pain rocketed through his brain, driving him back to the chair. He gasped for air, on the edge of black out, frozen in place until the sensation of his head spinning on its axis subsided. Head up, eyes open, he regained his feet with deliberate intent, promising himself to use this violation. He would find them. There was one more lesson to teach.

Divine retribution is a bitch.

At the pace his battered brain pan would allow, he began preparing himself to disappear. He cleaned the wound, showered the excess blood away, and assessed the damage. Massive headache. More nausea. Dizziness.

Concussion. No double vision. Mild.

Resisting the urge to pour another whiskey, he dipped into the medicine cabinet and popped a hydrocodone. He sorted through his shelf of facial hair coloring and spray tan, then moved to his closet, rummaging into the far reaches of his wardrobe.

Next up, he needed money for a flight out of Denver. Despite the attack, he still had resources. Not accustomed to the art of betrayal, the thief had missed a lockbox of credit cards, passports, and cash hidden under the floorboards. The box also held links to other bank accounts.

Two laborious hours later, the incessant throb in his head had retreated into the background. He examined his work in the full-length mirror. An oldster on holiday. One of several characters he had never road tested with the crew. Bland outfit of khaki, brown, green. Fake tan to accentuate any wrinkles. Full white beard. First-quality gray to white toupee covering his bandage. Tan fishing hat placed gingerly over the wound. He completed the outfit with a quad cane pulled from the upper shelf.

A man who wouldn't warrant a second glance.

He left nothing to chance. Relighting the fire and combing each room, he collected every piece of paper not carried on his person and carefully fed it into the fireplace. He resisted the temptation to watch it all burn.

The final touch of a chocolate brown down jacket and insulated gloves gave an old man protection from the elements.

He slung a modest travel bag over his shoulder and reluctantly bid farewell to his sanctuary. It had been more than wood and stone. The house provided a cushion of security unknown to him in those early years on his own.

He released a slow, easy breath and shrugged.

Everything and everyone was replaceable.

Time to go.

He left the compromised back door open, a welcome sign for the black bears, bobcats, and slim possibility of human scavengers that would destroy any remaining evidence of his existence. Without a look back, he tossed his bag in the cab of a diesel super-duty truck, powered up and, door to the four-car garage left as another open invitation to local intruders, plunged through the nearly unpassable banks of snow, wipers full-on.

He paused at the creek and pitched the house keys and garage opener into the bitterly cold water. Ten minutes down the winding trail to the main road, he found the slip stream of a DOT snow plow and followed it down the mountain.

~~~

I woke to the grim warning of a dirty gray morning. The mouthwatering smell of buttermilk pancakes had infiltrated my dreams, accompanied by the not-so-delectable voice of Goodman in my ear.

"Get up. The truckers loaned us their shower room. Clean up, grab a pancake, and meet us out front in fifteen minutes." He tossed my bag on the floor and threw me a fire engine red rain parka on the booth; no accident it was in blaring contrast to his conservative midnight blue Des

Moines Police Department trench coat. "You'll want this. It's gonna be a nasty day."

I struggled to my feet.

He stroked the fresh razor burn on his neck. "By the way, I like your dad." End of discussion. He plodded toward the exit.

Dad!

The blinking light on my phone let me know I'd slept through a text.

Belinda.

Let J.R. know all are safe. Yes, I am the best.

Fully awakened by my neglect of the man who, these days, often put me foremost in his concerns, I scanned the dining room turned care center. Three people in the white coats that signified medical staff were directing people traffic. All but one of the field hospital beds was empty and the fleet of official vehicles outside the building had shrunk in size. The remaining staff moved as if all were operating off eight hours of quality sleep. Two students were wrapped in rain jackets and green mesh caps procured from the truck stop gift emporium. Seth was still out for the count, oblivious to the commotion.

The night restaurant manager zoomed through the dining room with the morning waitstaff, carrying trays of, not a dream, buttermilk pancakes and scrambled eggs for the first responders. They handed to-go bags to anyone on the way out the door to medical transport.

These people worked dusk to dawn so we could tell terrified families—your child is alive and safe.

I was moved to exceed my daily text limit before most sensible people are even up and about.

Dad. Sorry. We're all safe. Hugs to the gang.

Belinda. You are the best.

I reached into my pocket and felt the crinkle of Jill's note. I dialed her.

This is Jill Bennett's voicemail. Leave a message.

Still asleep. Or maybe in the shower.

"Jill, it's, uh, Hank. Anderson. Sorry. I got distracted. I'm still in Lake Manawa with Phil, working on a client situation. Anyway, thanks for the other night. I'll be in touch."

Thanks for the other night?

The lyrics for Sade's 80s classic *Smooth Operator* played in my head. In a sarcastic way.

Freshly brewed coffee seemed like the best remedy for an awkward start to the day. I took a hit and retreated to the shower room. Ten minutes later I was standing under the tent, munching on a rolled flapjack and working on my second cup. I joined Phil and the Goodmans while they surveyed an interesting weather pattern advancing from the west. Like myself, they looked a bit worse for wear. Encouraged by a bit of caffeine burst, I pointed myself at the Goodmans.

"Sergeant Randall Goodman." The lean patrolman offered his hand. "Older brother. To paraphrase the epic song by the Marshall Tucker Band, I took the highway."

"Family outcast." Dale slapped his sibling on the back. "Couldn't cut it with real law enforcement."

"One question, Sergeant," I said.

The younger Goodman rolled his eyes. He and I had played this game.

"Of course."

"How is it that you are assigned to this crime scene?"

His good-natured grin evaporated.

"I'm on Major Sunderman's team."

"And how did the state patrol get called to this crime scene?"

He shoved his hands into the pockets of the neon green rain jacket.

Uncomfortable.

"That's two questions." He turned to his younger brother. "I like this guy."

"You would." He sounded angrier than usual, deciding to answer for Randall. "Phil wouldn't return my calls, but he did manage to reach out to my brother to ask for backup."

I stayed with it.

"Why you, Sergeant?"

"Detective Evans called me. I've known Phil since he and Dale were in the academy together. He believed the vehicle filled with students was headed west, close to I-80 but working the back roads. This is our district. We received a report of a beat-up white van sitting in the area designated for truckers." He nodded toward the north parking lot. "Phil got here in a hurry and the Iowa State Patrol followed our mission, to protect the citizenry and clean up after the Des Moines Police Department."

I watched Randall set his feet before Dale thumped him in the chest. Randall shouldered his brother. I couldn't tell if they were goofing off or somebody was about to get hurt.

How many times have they done this?

We all heard Phil clear his throat from the far side of the tent. Major Sunderman exited a mobile command center vehicle packed with ISP decals. She had the carriage of an official who slept upright, buttoned-down and totally refreshed.

"Don't know how she does that," muttered the sergeant. He stood straight and wiped imaginary dirt from his rain gear.

"Good morning, men." She approached, examining the overcast sky with a trained eye. "We had good road conditions yesterday." She nodded at the elder Goodman. "But today is on track to be what we call a State Patrol kind of day, eh Sergeant?"

"Most definitely, Major."

Inside joke.

She turned to the younger brother.

"How about an update for all present, Detective."

We quickly learned that Kenton Braxton had been removed to the coroner's office during the night. The number of bullets someone pumped into the former criminal's body could have killed him many times over.

Rage? Fear? Psychosis?

A hodgepodge of prints decorated the van and were unlikely to yield any useful results. It was being towed to wherever vans used in crimes go to be further combed over and live out their sad lives. The media, who showed up overnight in heavily logoed vehicles topped with all manner of antennas and discs, had interviewed anyone available who was vaguely connected to the events at hand. From our end, they'd been given the standard line—we are pursuing all leads. This told me we had no idea of the killer's whereabouts. The killer presumed to be Emma.

Phil added his report. The families of the students had been contacted. Most of them had been transported to a nearby Omaha hospital to reunite with family and make plans for ongoing physical and emotional care. The rest were headed in that direction.

"Except Seth," the major interrupted. "If we can impose upon you, Mr. Anderson, Seth's fragile condition and the connection you have formed with him leads me to a special request from his parents."

"No problem, Major."

"I haven't asked you yet."

"You'd like me to stay with him during transport to the city." It was an easy guess. "Happy to help."

I was fascinated by the major's ability to project respect and irritation simultaneously.

"You and Detective Evans," she corrected. "Thank you. I will, as they say, owe you one."

"He will likely need to collect on your favor at some point in the future, Major," Phil interjected.

Phil teasing me among his peers?

I looked at him for any hint of a smile. Nothing.

It was the elder Goodman's turn.

"Sergeant," she ordered. "You are charged with coordinating wrap-up at this location. The people here have been wonderful and we will leave this place better than we found it."

"Yes, Major." He nodded toward the window. "The restaurant and remaining EMS staff are already rollin' on it."

"Maybe you can call upon the kindness of family to assist," she said.

"Will do, Major." The detective didn't sound excited about his next assignment.

The major didn't say what she had assigned herself to. I assumed it was important.

By the time Phil and I made it inside to collect Seth, he was awake and dressed in a fresh supply of better fitting painter's pants and bright blue rain parka, covering a t-shirt with Grant Wood's vision of 30s Iowa farm life, the iconic American Gothic, on the front, courtesy of management. He'd worked a brush through his hair and was earnestly attacking a plate of pancakes and eggs.

"Morning Seth," I hailed. "How you feeling?"

He raised a finger to hold us while he chewed. "Morning," he gulped. "Stronger than yesterday. The doctor told me they got the results and can confirm we've all been drugged, which explains a lot." His face took on a thoughtful seriousness unrecognizable when compared to the young man I'd met three days previous. "No more dreams about hurting anyone. I did hear from Melinda, the paramedic, that you and Detective Evans will be giving me a ride to meet my parents at the hospital. I wouldn't mind the company."

A choir of phones vibrated.

"My parents." Seth wobbled to his feet and stepped away. "Hey, Mom."

"Good morning, dear," Phil said. It was Catherine. "Yes, I'm fine. Dale and Hank are right here with me."

"Jill." I moved toward the corner.

"Do I need to put on my lawyer suit and bail you out of another jam?" She sounded genuinely concerned.

"No," I said. "But you could put on the uniform and text me a picture."

Her laugh was better than a jolt of caffeine.

"It's a long story. I don't have time to tell you right now."

"One more thing and off you go, then."

"Yes."

"I liked your voicemail, Anderson. Stay safe."

I was still smiling at the blank screen when my attention came back to the matter at hand. Outdoors, the billboard-sized American flag flapped fiercely over the truck stop, framed against an increasingly threatening sky. Strands of rain began to hit the parking lot, a preview of the hammering downpour that would soon angle to the ground and drench the unprepared. Even indoors, my body could sense the drop in temperature, trained by a lifetime of harsh Midwestern autumn days.

I gave a final wave of thanks to the first responders, uniformed and not, parted the doors and got smacked by a blast of moist air, the harsh scent of oil melding with the contact high of gas splashed on concrete. No great mystery. The major had called it a State Patrol kind of day. The rest of us call it a miserable day for a drive. I stopped to watch the caravan of semis on high alert, grinding gears east in hopes of outrunning the storm, or west in hopes of anything better than an ice-skating rink with an invisible center line. Watching the collision of rough weather and commerce, my thoughts boomeranged back to the mysteries that remained in my part of the world.

Emma. Taranis. Dad.

What was J.R. hiding?

My imagination compiled a short list of the worst possibilities.

Stalled in my head, I missed out on the decision that Goodman would head for home after working as his brother's assistant. Phil and I would give Seth a lift into Omaha, keep him company until his parents hit town, then hightail it back to Des Moines to be embraced by the loved ones who were probably busy assembling the key elements of our misadventure. If this reality disturbed Phil, it didn't show. He had resurrected the unflappable demeanor I now understood to be part genuine Phil and part visual armor, built to contain his sorrow and anger.

Rain slapped pavement as we loaded our bags from the protection of the service station canopy. Goodman wished Seth good health and motioned me to the side. He closed the space between us, to compete with the ricochet of rain drops on sheet metal.

"My AA sponsor tells me I need to work on gratitude," he said. "Thanks for coming along."

I set myself for the punch line.

"And if you tell anybody you and I know outside the anonymity of a 12-Step meeting that I said something nice to you, I'll deny it."

I knew the temptation to go in for a handshake would torpedo his rookie attempt at civility.

"Your secret's safe with me, Detective."

He rotated and went in search of Randall, forgoing his usual mocking retreat.

"Mr. Anderson." The major, bad weather gear zipped up, hat with rain cover in place, called me over while Phil settled Seth into the back seat.

"Major Sunderman, I'd like to thank you for allowing me to be an honorary, temporary, voluntary part of the State Patrol team," I said.

Her face radiated something new to our brief acquaintance. Humor. "I would like to thank you for bringing your expertise and unique style to a terrible circumstance that could have become a catastrophic event."

"You run a tight operation." I returned the compliment. "Can I ask one more question?"

"My first name is Elizabeth, not Major." She beat me to it. "Now, I have a question for you. Is getting under people's skin useful in your line of work?"

A psychic cop?

"Sometimes it brings truth to the surface, Major. Sometimes."

She looked over my head, directly into the pebbles of ice beginning to join with the cloudburst. "Well, you appear to have refined the skill." Her steel grey eyes came back to me, full of honest concern. "You be careful out there, Hank."

With Seth tucked in, I assumed the passenger position. Phil drove west, across the Nebraska state line, then north, maxing out the defrosters for the drive to the hospital. Traffic slowed to a crawl. The wipers did battle with a sheen of freezing rain beginning to layer the windshield. He took the extra time to make good on our promise and gave Seth an edited summary of recent events, wisely omitting Braxton's death.

"I thought Emma was my friend until she showed up at the motel," Seth said. "She told me to call her Emma, not Sister Emma. I felt special. I'm such a geek."

"She's an exceptionally talented actor," I said.

"Why do I feel like it's my fault?"

"People like Emma, Musslewhite and Braxton want the folks they manipulate to blame themselves." It was too soon to facilitate a deeper understanding of her motives, or how vulnerable Seth had been.

"It's not my fault." He was tentative, taking the truth for a test drive.

"It may take a while for you to believe that all the way down to your socks."

"Which means you believe it all the way down to your socks." His pilot light had relit.

"You're a smart man."

Seth caught Phil's nod. The detective's agreement was absolute.

"I'll give it time," Seth said. He crossed his arms, folded into himself and closed his eyes. I watched while his breathing slowed and he did another rapid retreat into sleep, like an infant surrounded by too much clatter.

"End of session," I whispered.

A cautious forty-five minutes later, I caught sight of the hospital behind a now constant shroud of rain and sleet. The sliding stop and start from a traffic light woke Seth. He stared out the window. His view of the drab landscape did nothing to slow the anticipatory tap of his foot on the vinyl floor mat as we motored toward a side entrance.

Phil gave us our marching orders. "We've been provided with special parking in the ramp. Staff are just inside." He pointed toward the entrance. "I have a message that your folks have landed at Eppley Airport, Seth. The weather delayed their flight, but the car service will have them here within the hour."

Eager was the word that best fit our guy. He pulled open the door.

Phil slid to a stop. "Easy there. Your parents would be very unhappy if Hank and I got you all the way to

Omaha, and you crashed out on the ice. How about we stay dry and park in the ramp?"

A gust of wind caught the car door and swung it wide.

"I'll get out here." It appeared Seth's excitement had over-ridden his common sense. He went feet first out of the car and onto the sidewalk.

"I got this." I launched out the passenger side, sinking through the thin frozen crust at the curb. A stinging muck filled my running shoes.

Damn.

I managed to slam both doors, squish onto the slick concrete, and send Phil forward. I pulled the hood of the rain jacket over my head in a pitiful effort to compensate for ice-cold feet.

"Haaannnk!"

I spun in the direction of Seth's panicked scream, my peripheral vision blocked. He pointed through the rain. A black SUV had materialized, dodging in and out of parked cars, careening at highway speed through the slush, lights on high beam, its path in line to jump the curb where we stood. I reached and grabbed a fist full of his parka, throwing us to the side, into the grass. Momentum carried me face first into the sludge, the shock replaced by the soaked shriek of brakes at war with tires.

I rolled. My eyes were level with dripping wet tread an arm's reach from plowing us into the hospital lawn.

Not dead.

"Get up and get in!" A man's voice screeched through the squall.

Seth was on all fours at my side, pain and puzzlement mixed with the sleet beating against his face. "Levi?!" He looked through the windshield. "Emma!"

A slight man with a tawny, pockmarked face in a camo ball cap leaned through the open passenger window of the SUV, needing both hands to aim his gun, my red parka a first-class target through the storm.

"Get up!" he howled.

Seth was immobilized.

"NOW!"

Levi's rage sparked my fight system.

Buy time.

I forced myself to stand, pulling Seth's thin, quaking frame to my side. Soaked hair covered his face like strands of seaweed. He shuddered and I felt the weight of his ordeal fall into me.

"Another liar," I spat. I twisted my body toward the ramp and screamed. "PHIL!"

The big man launched through the archway. He broke into a sprint across the lawn, oblivious to the deluge, trench coat flapping, freeing his sidearm from a hip holster. "Police! Drop your weapons and get out of the car!"

The authority in his voice kicked my flight system into high. I locked arms with Seth.

"Run!" I spun and towed the two of us away from Levi. We skated across the crystalline lawn like drunks in a winter sack race. I heard the SUV jam into gear, tires fighting for purchase. A gun cracked.

"Whoomph! Whoomph! Whoomph!" The bullets embedded in something other than our bodies.

I thought I heard someone scream, "NO!"

Seth's unsteady gait gave out and he took another dive. I followed him down, arms linked, prepared for tire tracks to crush our backs. Phil barreled by.

"Stay down," he shouted.

I released Seth and rolled again. The SUV was in full throttle reverse. The front tires cleared the curb and bounced. The driver stood on the brakes and spun a grinding one-eighty. Narrowly missing a head-on collision with a light pole, our attackers weaved toward the outer road, tail lights fading into the veil of downpour. Phil help his position, gun out, until they disappeared.

Move.

I shivered to my feet. Phil holstered his weapon and lifted Seth without effort, the young man soaked to the bone, trembling from cold and terror. Phil shrugged out of his trench coat and placed it over Seth's shoulders. We all looked as if we'd showered fully clothed.

In short order, a host of people in rain gear shuffled from the entrance of the hospital and took over. Once certain we could move under our own power, they ushered Seth and me into the warmth, Phil covering our retreat. Despite dripping puddles onto the hospital carpet, Seth resisted the immediate suggestion of a hot shower and dry clothes. He was unmoved until Phil stepped up and handed him a cell phone.

"Somebody special wants to talk to you Seth."

"Hello." He could barely speak through his clattering teeth. He listened. "Yes Mom." He hung up and handed the phone back to Phil, managing a half-smile through blue-tinged lips. "Mom says do what the nurses say."

On cue, we were joined by the charge nurse, whose no-nonsense, compassionate energy reminded me of Juanita, my ER friend from the previous mess in the fall. A hospital security guard with a kind face and three heated blankets appeared, inviting me to help him stand watch at the staff locker room while my client dressed in another set of loaner duds, under Juanita's supervision.

"I'll be back." Phil headed down the hall, a trail of wet footprints behind him, the blanket an undersized cape. "I need to call this in."

The guard stayed within sight, grabbing me a chair and extra towels off a laundry cart. Answering an overhead page, he stuck his head into the locker room to let our guy know his parents had arrived. Seth made his way out, warmer and almost dry. He declined a ride in a wheelchair, holding the door open for me.

"You're next, Hank."

"Off we go, then." Juanita offered her hand to him. Under her watchful eye, the guard led them toward the nearest conference room.

Phil found me sitting alone in the locker room. I had no idea how long I'd been there.

"Seth's back in the arms of his family," he said. He handed me my overnight bag, having already changed from his water-logged clothes into a Des Moines Police sweatsuit. "I couldn't shoot. Too high risk in the open parking lot."

"No explanation necessary. As Captain America might say to the Black Panther, you arrived in the nick of time, my friend. I left my bullet-proof armor at home."

"Levi has terrible aim. All of the bullets went into the ground well behind the two of you."

"How about, you're welcome." I shook my head at his traditional over-the-top humility.

"You're welcome. I'll be outside. Thinking about which of us is Captain American and which is the Black Panther."

A joke? Twice in one day?

I managed to dress in the last clean outfit I'd packed without standing. The extra pair of warm socks was a bonus.

Call me Mr. Sensible.

I was comforted by the knowledge that Seth was reunited with his parents, in transition from courageous man who'd fought for his life to son who required the shelter of loved ones. I'd also had a theory pop into my head while sitting watch. I wanted to pass it on, but couldn't generate enough strength in my legs to get up from the bench.

"The Major is on the way," Phil leaned in the doorway. "With the Goodman brothers."

"I look forward to speaking with her as soon as I'm able to get to my feet without my knees buckling."

"Injury?" He joined me on the bench.

"Nothing you can see. But, I do believe my tank is near empty. I'd cry but I'm really sick of water."

"A therapist friend of mine says that may come later. Too much happened too fast to process it all right now."

I sat quietly with my personal police force until a touch of the numbness passed.

"I have a theory stirring."

"About Seth?"

"Yes."

"About why they keep coming for Seth?"

"Yes."

"I had another computer search done on him," he said. "It took some work but we found his pseudonym. Karter Griffin."

"Of course." A fact to back up my hypothesis.

Among the scores of interviews by professionals over the past four days, we had missed the possibility that all students were not created equal in the plan of whoever the hell was in charge of this horror story. Phil had determined that each student was from wealth, bilked for cash through group dues, camp registrations, incremental withdrawals from credit cards, and savings moved to ghost accounts, all of which were probably attached to the chief creep in what was turning out to be far more con game than cult.

But we had missed another essential truth.

There is rich and there is richer.

"Something I missed in our first session. Seth told me he mostly studied and did stuff with video games in his first semester at college."

Phil gave me space to think out loud.

"He didn't say he played video games. He said he studied and did stuff with video games," I repeated. Phil would have the next piece. "How rich is he?"

"Cliff Dwellers of Utopia, created by Karter Griffin, has been in the top five of video game sales for more than two years."

Sergeant Goodman stuck his bald, hatless head into the room before I got my next question out.

"Everybody's dressed," he said.

"I really didn't expect to see you men so soon." Major Sunderman marched through the doorway and handed Phil and I tall, capped cups of hot coffee. "From my private stash."

She removed her hat and laid it on the bench. I noticed for the first time that the major rocked a silver buzz cut under the official headgear. She stood with her hands folded behind her back as if holding briefings in shower rooms was standard protocol.

Got to be ex-military.

"Perhaps you can save young Oberstreet additional distress and give us the details of what happened. We'll need to ask him for anything specific he might remember, but with all he's been through, he doesn't need to replay the entire event for us."

She understands trauma.

"I can do that. After we fill in some blank spaces for you."

The sergeant stared wide-eyed as if I continued to test the patience of his boss in ways unimagined among the rank and file.

"What would those be?" She gave me more rope.

"We know why The Scholars of Calm took such a huge risk and came for Seth one more time."

She turned to Phil.

"Seth is much more than a confused young man from a wealthy family," he said. "He's the creator of a massively popular video game, The Cliff Dwellers of Utopia, released under the pseudonym, Karter Griffin. He's considered a prodigy in the gaming world."

"How rich is he?" The major and I were on the same wavelength.

"At the age of seventeen he became a millionaire, many times over. Since then, tens of millions more in sales."

"Holy hell." The sergeant spoke for the whole room.

"Until Seth turned eighteen, his money was protected in a trust. The family verified that by the time he went to college, he'd reached majority age and could access the money on his own."

"How famous is he?" She was asking the right questions.

"With some effort, his story, including his discomfort with public attention, can be found online," Phil added. "I believe The Scholars of Calm tracked him down and preyed on his vulnerability. They used the other kids for seed money and cover."

She finished his thought. "But Seth was the main target."

The major, not waiting for anyone to agree, resumed handing out assignments.

"Sergeant, I need you to take Hank's statement about the assault. Detective Evans, if you will accompany me to the family, we'll finalize arrangements to get our young genius home. Detective Goodman, I assume you will continue to work with my department on the search for Emma and Levi."

She reached for her hat. "I do have one more question."

She's learning my favorite game.

"How did these people know Seth was headed for this particular hospital?" She saw a room full of blank stares. "Give it some thought, men."

Phil needed every inch of his considerable stride to keep up with the major when she moved out the door.

―――

The motel had been within a stone's throw of an industrial park of vacant warehouses and businesses limping toward closure, with more than enough broken-down vehicles to conceal the SUV. They slept in shifts, Braxton's gun in hand. Not out of the fear for the cops who were pursuing them. Out of the fear that they would be robbed and murdered by the other desperate people marking time at this end of the road.

Levi stayed awake by locating the hospital and studying a map of the grounds.

They left at what should have been dawn, moving through the lifeless morning, settling in the back of a hospital parking lot with a full view of the front and side entrances, fog lights only. It was Levi who spotted the vague outline of a skinny guy with long hair in a blue parka crawling out of the back seat of a sedan. Oberstreet? A red parka was next. Short. The shrink.

"It's them."

When Emma punched the accelerator and switched to high-beams, she'd been certain The Fates had chosen them to win.

The sight of the giant cop coming at them through the rain changed all that. She couldn't hear his words, but she'd seen him pull his gun. Her boneheaded brother ignored her over the ear-splitting chaos of his finger on the trigger and sleet shot-gunning off the hood and windshield. He missed, all six shots. Sure the cop wouldn't miss, muscle memory told her to shove the SUV into reverse. She spun the wheel, vaulted back to the pavement, and floored it in 4-wheel drive as he leveled up. She'd expected to hear rear window glass shatter right before bullets blew through the seats and entered their bodies. She had no idea why he didn't fire.

Her fingers ached from her grip on the steering wheel by the time they parked in a cluster of cars at a big box store down the road. "Don't give me the gun. I might feel a need to find more bullets and use it on whoever is closest."

He was shaking too hard to lift it anyway.

"Now we have to run," she said.

There was no one in the car willing to risk reminding her whose plan had led them to this final option.

~~~

"Let's find a more comfortable place to sit," the sergeant suggested.

He pointed at the stately walnut door across the hall.

CHAPEL.

The door closed like a vacuum seal. The dimly lit prayer room provided an immediate respite from the insanity of the past three days, dampening the last charge of fuel supplied by my shower room insight. I sat in the small pew closest to the alter and lowered my head into my hands. Tears dripped through my fingers, noiseless on the carpet.

When I raised my head, the Goodmans were standing in uneasy silence.

"Those." I didn't know what to call them, sitting in a chapel.

"Lowlifes." The detective helped me out.

"Those lowlifes might have smashed us into the slush or gunned us down if Phil hadn't been there."

Gunned us down?

The detective's coat pocket fluttered and played *Birdland*, a welcome intrusion. He went back through the door to answer his phone. The sergeant stood watch until I straightened, back against the pew. He poured his height into the seat behind me, hat in hand. I took it as my cue.

"Seth and I got out of the car. He screamed. I saw the SUV coming at us. I pulled Seth to the ground. Levi waved a gun at us. He had a camo hat and long brown hair. Emma was driving. We stood. Phil ran out of the garage and pulled his gun. We ran. Levi shot at us. Phil put himself between us and them. They drove away."

He didn't record or write anything down.

"That's good. All I need."

He knows trauma, too.

Goodman the Elder and I sat and watched the oval stained-glass window above the altar reflect hues of blue, yellow and sea green. On another day I'd have interrogated him about his brother. He seemed comfortable with the quiet.

The door to the chapel whooshed open for Phil. "The Omaha PD found a beat-up black late model SUV with plates that didn't match the VIN in a parking lot off

32nd Street," he said. "No doubt, they've stolen another car. They might still be in the area."

"Thanks for getting on this." The other Goodman followed him in and hung up. "Call from home. Debra Stanwyck and Calvin Tracy. There were distinguishable prints on empty cereal boxes in a partially burned garbage pile at the farm, but they weren't in the system."

He leaned over and slapped his brother on the back.

Friends again?

"Randall had a hunch. Check juvenile records. Sister and brother, three years apart, different fathers. Multiple minor arrests. Closed records, until now. Approximately ten years ago they ran away from a residential facility and disappeared. No school records. No adult arrests. Mother long gone. Both fathers deceased."

Children raised by the state.

I felt a jolt of sorrow for the criminals we now knew were siblings.

The next cop in the door was the major. "Men, we have another change, requested by the parents." She took her hat off, aiming it at the brothers. "I've spoken with a lieutenant from the Des Moines Police Department, who I sense knows the Goodmans quite well."

The brothers looked like they'd been caught sneaking extra cookies.

She's definitely psychic.

"He has cleared the detectives to escort the Oberstreets to the airport, for security purposes."

"Detectives only?" I wasn't pleased.

"Plus, Victor Segura, their security chief and the private security agent who drove them to the hospital. Given the events of the day and the lengths to which these individuals are willing to go in pursuit of their goals, I am instructing you to stand down, Hank."

"Instructing, not asking." I didn't have enough filter left to cover my frustration. "I'll give you points for precision, Major. You chose your command words carefully."

She didn't flinch. "I appreciate all you have done and been through in the past several days. But no, this is not a negotiation."

Maybe it was a sign of growth; I took stock of how far out beyond her strict professional lines Major Sunderman had already colored on behalf of the Des Moines contingent and reeled myself in.

"Don't forget to come back for me, detectives."

Our band of law enforcement professionals dropped me in an employee break room, with hot soup for company, while they finalized the details of Seth's release home and coordinated the search for the elusive siblings. My synapses were stirring with a consistency similar to the murky bowl of French Onion staring back at me.

A few slurps later the glass door swung open and in came Seth, finally decked out in his own clothes, skinny black jeans, black tee, and unbuttoned red-on-black flannel shirt, his hair shining past his shoulders. His face showed the strain of the ordeal, but his skin was at least three shades rosier than the ghostly pallor of our first and most recent experiences. He was ushered in by a well-coifed woman who could have been his identical twin if born twenty-some years earlier and a sun-weathered, fireplug of a man who might have been a ranch hand if his hand-tooled cowboy boots, pressed jeans, and starched white pearl-buttoned shirt weren't worth more than my entire wardrobe. Behind them came a compact, stone-faced Hispanic man, his loose-fitting Colorado Rockies pullover and blue jeans doing little to hide what Dad calls, "a man with muscles on his muscles."

"Mr. Anderson." My Midwestern manners kicked in and I struggled to my feet. The woman flowed to the end of the table and threw her arms around me. "I don't have words for how grateful we are for all you've done for our Seth."

She stood back, then embraced me again. My arm complained, but my heart felt the all-encompassing sensation of a mother's love. While her tears trickled onto my last clean shirt, the man who had to be Seth's dad reached around her and thrust out his hand, shaking mine with a grip that undoubtedly wielded a hammer long before it signed paychecks as the CEO of Oberstreet Construction.

"Mom. Dad." Seth sounded like a normally embarrassed son.

The parents stepped back. The man reaching into his pocket and handed his wife a blue bandana-style handkerchief.

"I'm Wyatt."

Of course, you are.

"This is Seth's mother, Ava." He sounded like he was lucky to know her. "And our Chief of Security, Victor Segura," he added, pointing to the other man, who gave an almost imperceptible greeting and positioned himself at the door.

I flashed on another Victor I'd known.

Security?

"We do a lot of work for the state and federal government." Wyatt guessed my question. "It's a tough business with tough people."

Taking in the whole scene, I was certain Wyatt and Victor could hold their own.

"Victor warned us that Seth's notoriety could put him at risk." Wyatt's eyes radiated guilt. "I didn't take him seriously enough." Victor's face revealed no visible sign of judgement. "When we finally realized Seth was missing, we contacted the police. Victor activated his cyber security team. He said, if someone was after Seth's money then..." Wyatt's words caught in his throat.

"I understand." I did. If The Scholars of Calm had accessed Seth's money, they would have had no further need for him.

Seth edged toward the security chief.

He understands, too.

"I can't believe we let him go with those evil people." Ava's pain was heart-wrenching. "We're not wide-eyed fools."

"Mom." Seth's loving impatience told me they'd already had this conversation. I was sure they would have it again. He turned to me. "What would you say, Mr. Anderson?

"I would say you all have a lot to talk about and plenty of time to do that talking, folks. I would also tell you I have never encountered a group of better liars or manipulators."

And I've met some pros.

A side glance from Victor let me know he'd made the same determination.

"Let's give Seth a chance to say goodbye, Ava." Wyatt was clearly not a man who stood around much. My gut told me his self-disclosure was out of character and he was ready to move on. He pulled an ornate pocket watch from his pressed jeans and looked out the wall of windows.

"This is Colorado weather without the mountains. We've got to go if we're going to make the flight home."

Ava straightened her shoulders and led her husband to the door. She stopped to brush a piece of lint off her son's shirt, as if making sure he was really there.

"I forgot," she said. "I'm so happy you were not harmed, Hank. Get home to your family as soon as you can." Her gracious smile made me think of my own mom.

"I'll be outside, man." Victor cuffed Seth on the shoulder like a big brother on the lookout for bullies to pummel, and followed the parents.

Seth shuffled his laced boots. "Sorry about my parents. They can be a little over the top."

"I like them a lot. I can only imagine how thrilled they are to be taking you home."

"Almost as excited as I am to be going with them." He looked beyond me, into his recent past. "Not harmed, Mom said. There are many kinds of harm, aren't there." He came back to eye contact. "Can I check in and let you know how I'm doing?"

"I hope you will."

"Thank you sounds pretty weak after what we've been through."

"My dad would say, seeing you on your feet awake and alive is more good news than any one person deserves in a day."

He straightened his shoulders and moved to the door.

Like mother, like son.

"You could do me one favor," I said.

He stopped. "Anything."

"I think we've arrived at the point in our work when it's entirely appropriate for you to call me Hank."

"Hank." He tried it on for size. "I forgot one thing. They told me you won't be with the police escorting us to the airport. I'd feel better if you were there all the way to the gate."

"Sorry. Official orders."

He scratched his chin fuzz. "Thanks again, Hank."

Watching him go, I was thrilled that Seth had rejoined his family. I just couldn't isolate the one feeling among the rush of emotions tumbling through me.

~~~

I am standing in a newly plowed field, dressed in full Hazmat suit, ice pellets the size of skipping stones sticking to my visor, blocking my vision. I sense, rather than see, the people huddled under a battered willow tree in the distance, certain that if I can get to them we will all live through the storm. I fight to lift my arm and wipe the face shield. Nothing. My hands are anchored to the sides of the protective gear as hail attaches to the suit, forming layer upon layer of magnetized weight. Struggling to push forward, my knees buckle and I am slowly driven to the ground, face down. Inexplicably, I am immobilized, yet feel no fear. I am annoyed. By a relentless buzzing in my ears.

An unyielding noise wrenched me out of a cavernous sleep, head resting on my arms, folded on the table. I pushed to my elbows, disorientated by the dream.

"I fell asleep," I said to no one. My phone danced on the pressed wood surface. "I should answer."

"Marlowe?"

"Dennis."

"Where are you?"

"I think I'm in the break room at a hospital in Omaha."

"You think?"

"I just took an impromptu nap and I'm either talking to my partner, or I'm still dreaming."

"Catherine must have heard from Phil. She called Belinda, who called me, who's calling you. She said more craziness went down. I wanted to hear your voice and know you landed intact."

"Then it is a dream."

"Smart ass. Seriously, how are you?"

"After my client and I were nearly run down by a marauding grifter turned murderer, then shot at by the person we now know is her brother, I'm exhausted down to my toes and my stomach tells me I need to eat, then throw up."

"Understandable. Better than horrible, far worse than good."

"Exactly."

I stood to look through the bank of windows. "I don't know what your weather is like, but over this way a pair of ice skates and a tail wind are the preferred mode of transportation. We might not make it home tonight."

I heard someone talking in the background. "Jerry says the storm that hit Omaha is racing toward us through desolate cornfields full of right-wing homophobes as we speak."

Jerry is an urban Chicago native who came to Des Moines to play basketball for Drake University, met Dennis, and stayed. He enjoys using phrases like "desolate cornfields" and "right-wing homophobes" when he references my place of origin.

Goodman the Younger filled the doorway, wagging a finger at me. "Message from the major, Dr. Franklstein."

Victor Frankl. Still my hero. Goodman. Still a jerk.

"I've got to go," I said. "Let the gang know I'm holding my own. Thanks for checking in." I hung up.

Phil followed close behind. He tossed me an anonymous gray, lined rain jacket. Size small. "The major and the sergeant are back on the road. Highway crews are out in full force but the interstate has patches of black ice all the way to DeSoto. The highway is shut down at Adair due to several tractor trailer accidents."

I flashed on my new trucker friend, Mabel, hoping she pulled into a rest stop to sit out the madness. "This is important to me because?"

"The major sent us back with another change in assignments. Seth Oberstreet has made a personal request. He wants you to accompany Dale and me in the lead vehicle to the airport. He says it will bring symmetry to his rescue from The Scholars of Calm."

Seth has clout.

I retrieved my shoes from the heating vent by the door. They were almost dry.

"What were the major's exact words?"

I had never before seen Phil display a smile large enough to show his sparkling teeth. "She would appreciate your cooperation with this change and looks forward to seeing us all in the future, but not the near future."

"I may have to start a Major Sunderman fan club."

On this leg of our perpetual road trip, I was the back seat passenger. The detectives rode in silence, checking the rear and side mirrors to keep the midnight blue Escalade carrying the Oberstreets in view on the sparsely traveled streets through Omaha. Phil drove with utmost care, north on 24th, passing Creighton University. The glowing steeple of St. John's Church reached into the gloom. The sidewalks were flowing with students, carrying Bluejay backpacks, several in gym shorts, undeterred by the weather. A right turn on Cuming brought us close to the university baseball stadium, the long-standing site of the College Baseball World Series, before we faded onto Abbott toward Eppley.

Bundled in my new coat, the defroster on full, my eyelids fluttered in the direction of another nap.

"Dale."

I felt Phil tap the brakes and steer into the car's slide, tires failing to grip ice. My eyes popped open and I twisted to catch a maroon, sleet and sand splattered compact outpace the Escalade from the passing lane and swerve to the right, crowding into the space between our vehicles. Phil caught pavement and steered plumb with the lane. Foot off the gas, we slowed. Without breaking speed, the driver of the compact veered left. Goodman was out the car door, gun in hand, by the time Phil rolled us to a stop, lowered his window, and cleared his weapon.

The kid leaning out the passenger side of the open window had both middle fingers displayed as his only weapons when they passed. His expression flipped from hostile grin to terror, his scream competing with the whine of their engine when his buddy floored it. Weaving out of control, they slid sideways through a red light, inches from barreling into a line of parked cars before grabbing the road and bolting west, further into the city.

Goodman was breathing heavy when he holstered his gun and sunk back into car.

"I'm sorry I over-reacted, men." Phil said. He holstered his weapon, put the car back in gear, and pulled into a slot at an empty Chinese takeout joint on the corner.

"Hey, I thought it was the siblings, too," Goodman said.

"Hank."

"No longer sleepy, Phil."

"How about you and I regain our composure by checking on the family. Dale, will you step back out and stay with the car."

"Sure."

Phil got out and opened my door.

I leaned and was tugged back into place by the seatbelt. I clicked the latch, my hand shaking, grateful that I remembered to step over a puddle of slush.

Danny, the driver of the Escalade was a professional. When he saw the compact change lanes, he'd managed to duck into an auto repair lot a few yards back. He parked behind a commercial dumpster, engine running, handgun out.

Victor stepped from the back side of the dumpster, an arms-length section of metal pipe in his gloved hand. He made eye contact with me. "No guns allowed on the flight over."

"Thanks, men. Sorry I over-reacted," Phil repeated.

"Hey, twenty years on the job, Detective," Danny said. "Two people in the car. No report on what vehicle the bad guys stole next. The driver squeezed between us. I'd have done the same."

Victor dropped his makeshift weapon back into the dumpster and glided toward the back seat.

"Anyway, we had these folks covered." Danny slid his gun into a shoulder holster under his black suit jacket. "And I do have a permit."

I poked my head in the driver's side and peeked into the two-row back seat. Ava was whispering into her husband's ear. Seth was in row three, sleeping. "All clear, folks." I gave them my—it ain't no big deal—smile. "The more sleep the better."

"What the hell happened?" It was clear Wyatt was used to being in the know.

I put my finger to my lips. "Nothing at all. The detectives thought they saw a suspicious car, but it was nothing at all." Old therapy technique. Reassure, then repeat.

"Then let's get back on the road." Ava elbowed him. "No offense intended. Sometimes my mouth gets ahead of me."

"None taken, Wyatt. You're a man trying to get his family home."

Ava graced me with a high voltage smile, payment in full for my diplomacy.

I saw Victor put eyes on his charge. His shoulders relaxed at the sight of Seth, unaware of another near-miss. He tucked himself back into the Escalade.

"Let's roll, people." I waved my hand forward and started back to the car.

Danny barked a laugh. "He thinks he's funny."

"Yes," Phil said. "Please don't encourage him."

"Put some hustle in it, Detective Evans." I projected enough for Goodman to hear. "The brave and nimble Detective Goodman has caught his breath and these folks have a flight to catch."

Score one, Anderson.

Phil led us back onto the street for an uneventful couple of miles before we merged into the quagmire of traffic maneuvering to enter the weather-bound airport. He had time to give us the lay of the land.

"We'll park in the passenger drop-off zone. Victor looked things over when he arrived with Seth's parents. It provides the shortest route into the terminal. He and I will escort the family." He caught my attention in the rearview mirror. "Dale and Danny will have eyes on the entrance and watch for trailing vehicles. Hank, I need you to stay in the car. Agreed?"

"Agreed."

It wasn't necessary to tell him I'd already determined Seth wouldn't benefit from another long goodbye.

He pulled into a diagonal space with a spot open on his left. The Escalade filled it. The crossing lane to the first floor of the Central Terminal was packed with foot traffic. Phil stepped from the car and flashed his ID at the airport security officer strolling by. Their conversation was brief. Goodman and Danny moved out to have a full view of the scene. In sequence, Victor exited, opened the rear passenger doors, extracting Ava and a sleepy-eyed Seth. The crowd seemed to part naturally, Phil's bulk in front, Victor's on the left. Wyatt trailed behind, operating as the rear guard. Seth hesitated as the doors slid open. Wyatt rested a hand on his son's shoulder and walked him into the terminal.

The entire operation was over in less than two minutes. I wondered if anyone else's heart beat like a bass drum until the door closed behind the family.

Goodman and Danny remained on alert until Phil returned. The detectives shook hands with the driver, who passed them a business card. He led us out of the airport and gave a two-fingered salute in his mirror before turning off.

"We escorted the family to security. Victor will call me when they board," Phil said. "Could be a while."

"Which means we're going to stay close until we know the family is in the air?"

"Yes."

I motioned toward the deepening gloom.

"I did my due diligence and called home," he added. "I agreed with Catherine that we should not drive into the heart of the storm in light of our recent history."

On the road to making better decisions.

"Instead, we're going to drive to a local diner that Dale has raved about on many occasions. We will eat a hot meal, after which we will find a decent hotel with large, soft beds. We'll head home tomorrow. Early."

There was no argument from the troops.

In familiar Midwestern fashion, the sun, which had not made an actual appearance during the day, receded into the horizon. Partially melted streets cleared by the city's formidable highway department were sure to refreeze in the fade to night. Goodman pointed the way and landed us at our destination. A brilliant blue neon sign burst through, calling out one of my favorite welcomes, DINER. It was secured atop a silver metallic rectangular box shining through the urban dreary. We unfolded from the car and Goodman led us heads down through the cold, in the entrance, aiming directly for a blue vinyl corner booth with a steamed window view.

We hung our jackets on the hooks provided at the end of the table and soaked in the fragrant greeting of home-cooked food before depositing ourselves on the squeaky blue cushions. The table was set with detailed placemat menus. I'd seen Goodman eat and put faith in his declaration that we'd been given passage into diner heaven.

The place certainly looked the part. Symmetrically lined booths. Matching blue circular stools perched on chrome along a bright white Formica countertop sitting on a black and white checkerboard linoleum floor, slightly worn by years of customers flowing in and out. An open window into the cook's station encouraged us to watch the autopilot movements of two fry cooks knocking out the meals with shouts of, "Order Up!"

The come on in and take a seat ambience was topped off with a gallery of signed photos from local celebrities decorating the wall behind a vintage cash register. I recognized Bob Gibson, the legendary St. Louis Cardinals pitcher, and Buddy Miles, drummer, guitarist, and vocalist extraordinaire, who played with everybody from Hendrix to Santana and wrote the before my time funk classic *Them Changes*.

It was a bonus to see both detectives peruse the top portion of the menu, adhering to Hank's First Rule of Diner Eating:

Regardless of the time of day, eat breakfast.

I'd been raised in places like this. I loved it.

Lucinda, as advertised by her clip-on name badge, showed up with a fresh pot of coffee, three white ceramic mugs, and a personality that obliterated the ruthless day. She lent authenticity to this special world, the crisp pale blue waitress uniform of times gone by a marvelous palette for her perfect 70s Afro and fingernails matching the white, black, and blue of the restaurant furnishings.

"Good to see you, Dale." She filled his cup first. "I see you brought some tired and hungry friends with you."

"Good to see you, too, Lucinda." Goodman's greeting was a level of polished interest unknown in the time I'd spent with the man. "This is my partner, Detective Evans, and." He searched for words. "Our colleague, Hank Anderson."

"I know what Detective Dale likes." Our server smiled her appreciation for a customer who embraced the diner experience, and maybe more. "If you gentlemen put your trust in Lucinda, I will bring you a meal designed to fill your stomach, sooth your soul, and lift your spirits."

I wanted to say—Amen—but it didn't fit the general mood of the table.

We ate family style from platters of four-egg fresh veggie and Swiss omelets, banana-coconut pancakes, pork sausage links spiced with red pepper and made in-house, perfectly crisp hand-shredded hash browns, cornbread with honey butter, and bottomless cups of excellent coffee. The only words that broke through were, "Thank you" and "Perfect."

Satiated, we leaned back into the booth. My plate looked as if a hungry mutt had worked it over.

Lucinda cleared the table. "Young man, you acquitted yourself quite well considering your somewhat smaller stature."

"Professional eater, Lucinda. I grew up in the restaurant business."

If possible, her face lit up one more notch. "Are you, by chance, any relation to J.R. Anderson?"

"My dad."

"Well, isn't that lovely." I was accustomed to having J.R. known far and wide among restaurant people. "He's a fine plain-spoken man."

Not a fine fellow restauranteur?

"Which makes you eligible for a piece of the best blackberry rhubarb pie in all the state of Nebraska, maybe the whole country." She sped off to the kitchen with a wink and an aura of purpose. In less time than I needed to grasp ahold of another Saturday surprise, she reappeared with three enormous slices of pie, a scoop of hand-churned vanilla ice cream resting next to each.

I pointed at the multi-colored sign holding court over the order window:

FAMILY DINING BY FAMILY SINCE 1972

"I couldn't help but notice we're the only table you're serving, Lucinda." The counter and at least a dozen booths were under the care of two women and one man moving like a choreographed jazz dance, taking care of hardy customers whose appetites had eclipsed the lousy driving conditions.

"You caught me, Hank." She nudged me a bit further into the booth with her hip and joined us. "My parents opened this place in '72. I've done it all. Food prep. Cook." She pointed a high-gloss fingernail at the pie. "Bake. Took the place over when I got myself clean and the folks retired."

Clean?

There it was. Dad liked the variety of driving to Omaha to catch an occasional Alcoholics Anonymous meeting. I looked at Goodman, who gave me a blank stare, holding true to the principle of anonymity for members of the fellowship.

"I like to serve special customers." She patted the table in front of Goodman. "It reminds the youngsters on my staff that I still got it. Now, less talking, more eating. Let me see you manly men take a bite of pie. Then you can tell me how wonderful I am."

Every rural kid knows cows have multiple stomachs. Not to be outdone by the big guys, I pretended to be part Holstein.

Lucinda left us to greet other customers, or, as dad and mom described it, "work the room." We were debating the merits of one more coffee refill versus finding a motel for a post-banquet nap when Phil's phone rang.

Boarding the plane.

"Detective Evans." He plucked the bill from the table. "No problem." He looked at the oval clock on the far wall. "I'll ask Hank."

He muted.

"Victor?"

"Ava Oberstreet. Their flight to Denver is further delayed. The airport is packed with noisy, tired travelers. Seth says he's fine."

"But they'd like us to come."

I pressed my face close to the window on my right and wiped the moisture away. A public works truck was scraping close to the concrete and spreading more high-tech de-icing on the road. A hint of starlight in the west gave off a good news, bad news kind of vibe. Although the worst of the storm had rotated beyond Omaha, the wind and cold had taken up residence for the night. Goodman's weather app told us the trailing snow was stalled over the prairie, but treacherous streets were certain to force an all-night fight for the local road crews.

I gave a thumbs up.

Phil un-muted. "Traffic is still slow, Mrs. Oberstreet. We'll be there as soon as possible."

We shrugged into our coats. Lucinda checked us out at the register, proving she could in fact do every job in the place. She walked us to the exit. At the door she handed Goodman a sandwich-sized container.

"The pie was on the house. The homemade cinnamon roll is for a late-night snack, Detective Dale." She rested her hand on his forearm in a way that meant they were more than AA buddies. "Come back and see me soon."

"You're the best." He laid his hand on top of hers.

Phil centered his hat, palm on the crown before stepping into the wind.

"You men be careful out there. You say hi to J.R. from Lucinda, Hank. Lucinda from Omaha."

I bid a cheerful goodbye to the best part of our day.

I'll do that, Lucinda. Right after I find out what he's hiding from me.

Gentlemen all, Phil and I did not ask questions about the Goodman-Lucinda connection. In turn, he had the wherewithal not to brag on the fact that he was in possession of the only cinnamon roll. I did decide to keep Lucinda's pet name, Detective Dale, in my back pocket for use down the road.

Retracing our route, I stared longingly when we cruised through the 13th Street intersection to the Old Market.

Note to self. Schedule field trip to Homer's Record Store in the Old Market. On a sunny day. Invite Jill.

This time, we followed the signs for short-term parking at Eppley, then made our way past ticketing, onto the escalators to the upper level. Seth and his parents had backtracked from security into a triangular corner beyond the food court in the South Terminal. Wyatt was on alert and caught our attention. Victor was on his feet and on his phone, scanning the football-field shaped room as he listened. Seth stopped pacing and snaked his way through the crowd.

"You guys didn't have to go to this trouble. Mom and Dad got worried when our flight was delayed for the third time." His hyper-scrutiny of the milling throng suggested his parents were on target.

"How about you and I take Detective Evans for a walk, Seth?"

The young man got right with it. "If it'll help him relax, I'm all for it."

"I just had a big meal," Phil rubbed his ironing board belly. "A short walk would be excellent."

Goodman didn't need any input to know his job was to sit with the parents and stay in touch with Victor on the flight situation. He wasn't a great conversationalist, but he had spent a couple of decades getting criminals to talk.

The multitude parted as our improvised support group—retro hipster, slightly disheveled suburbanite, and super-sized man in police sweats—found its way to three seats in a semi-quiet nook tucked past the obligatory chain newsstand. Pop music retreads played over the tin-can airport sound system, interrupted by repetitious announcements of weather-induced gate changes and flight delays. Less than ideal, but the distractions of physical movement and our presence had a calming effect on Seth.

"I'm sorry I didn't tell you I was rich." It was hard to know if he was apologizing for his omission or for being a wealthy computer whiz. "So many people treat me different when they find out who I am. The first time I met you, Hank, my brain was so scrabbled, it didn't even occur to me."

"Video game inventor." Phil deftly shifted gears. "Way out of my wheelhouse."

The diversion worked. Seth launched into a passionate discourse on the magical and lucrative world of gaming. I noticed a slight tremor when his hands punctuated the lecture. He caught me looking.

"I get a little wound up when I talk about this stuff. Victor's the only one who gets it."

"Victor's a gamer?"

"Definitely!" Seth was a fan. "Victor's a Cyber Science guy. Air Force Academy. He never talks about what he did for the Air Force before he went private."

A poke from my old friend curiosity was derailed by another call to Phil.

"Yes. Excellent. We missed it. We'll head your way." He hung up. "Detective Goodman says they made an announcement. Your connecting flight is in the air. You'll be on your way home sometime this evening."

The young man's smile didn't match the concern in his eyes.

"Seth?"

"I'm a little nervous about being on an airplane, Hank. Small space and all."

"I've got something for you." I reached into my pocket and set the extra notepad I'd commandeered from Phil in Seth's open palm. "On the way over, I wrote down some skills to practice on the plane. A simple exercise to regulate your breathing. Self-talk technique to calm your mind. A relaxation app you can load on your phone and listen to. The most helpful pastime might be listening to your parents talk for a couple of hours about how glad they are to be taking you home."

"That should either calm me or put me to sleep."

It seemed like the first time I'd belly laughed in weeks.

～～～

After the disaster at the hospital, the plan became—get away as far as possible, as fast as possible, with as much of Taranis' money as the siblings could get their hands on. There was one particularly disturbing factor outside of their control. If Taranis was alive, he was high on the list of people they were running from. The possibility of a breathing Taranis, who would know she masterminded the double-cross, triggered an uncommon flicker of fear in Emma.

Ditching their weather-beaten vehicle in a strip mall beyond the hospital grounds, they walked in the cold, wordless, heads on swivels, to the nearest city park. Empty of the usual walkers and children, they broke the lock on the men's restroom and went into a familiar routine, changing their appearance with supplies each had jammed into their backpacks. Marginally encouraged by the lifting storm, they walked a few more blocks, deeper into a neighborhood on the cusp of gentrification. They needed a different, inconspicuous ride.

Remnants of the overcast day provided decent cover. An unlocked, sun-faded blue Ford that came off the line before anti-theft alarms became standard was parked at an angle, telling them the driver barely made it home, well over the legal limit. Aware of the potential for nosy neighbors, they didn't take time to swap plates.

Emma allowed herself to smile when her little brother did his magic. He started the car in seconds, without benefit of a key, and slid over the console. She climbed in and as quietly as the clunker's patched exhaust system would allow, hauled them off to find an out-of-the-way internet hotspot where Levi could use one more of his talents.

Parked behind an upscale coffee joint advertising its grand opening, the car's heater on high, Levi searched for flights south with any chance of being cleared for late departure. Courtesy of Taranis' network of off-the-books professionals, they had passports, with a stack of credit cards to match. Drawing from their list of bogus identities, the siblings booked the last two grossly overpriced first-class seats, non-stop to Houston. Once there, they would rent a car, ditch it at the border, and cross into Mexico.

It was a whole lot easier to get out of the country than it was to get in.

~~~

By the time Taranis made it beyond the city to Denver International he was certain the crew would decide to dump the students and split up. He'd taught them it was easiest and safest to work in twos. Levi would stick by Emma's side, as he always did. Braxton and Musslewhite protected one another all the way through prison. They were a team.

Where would they go?

An airport. Get as far away as they could, as fast as they could. Close, but not Des Moines close.

Omaha. Eppley. He was confident it was their next best choice. Catch a flight to Houston. Blend into the sea of people passing through the airport named for George H. Use fictitious passports and licenses. Rent a car. Leave it at the border and walk across at Matamoros. It was not the kind of place where affluent young tourists wanted to camp out for long, but they'd have more than enough money to wind their way to the more luxurious Yucatan, lost forever. In past briefings, it was what he titled—The Collapse of Civilization Plan.

The last question was his biggest gamble. Could he get to them before they disappeared?

The storm clouds to the east were clearing. The Denver airport would soon go full throttle with a precision born of frequent shifts in weather patterns. He would lose an hour with the time change, but the domino effect of flight delays could keep his people stuck well into the night.

His people. The words roiled in his gut. They weren't his anymore.

Taranis dropped the truck in a long-term parking lot overlooking the rolling meadows and Blue Mustang sculpture dominating the landscape beyond the terminal. Nicknamed Blucifer for its luminous red eyes, he allowed himself a moment to reflect on the statue. He'd read that a section of the horse fell on the artist during its creation, resulting in the man's death. Casting aside the temptation of an ironic leap to the death of his own master plan, he pulled out his extra burner and found available seats to Omaha, probably vacated by business people who decided not to fly into the eye of the storm.

Flight secured; he reviewed the steps of his preparation. The diesel's registration was ashes. The plates were out of state. He'd be in Mexico before anyone realized the pristine truck was an abandoned vehicle. Satisfied, he assumed his new persona, friendly, unmemorable, and boarded a quiet shuttle.

The airport was scurrying back toward business as usual. He expected to wait, as the airlines dealt with the shuffle of flights behind the storm's advance into the Midwest. The drugs he'd taken to manage his pain dampened his appetite, but he forced himself to eat a bowl of chicken soup to maintain his energy and fill his time.

Navigating the terminal was easy. Even with the long lines and hours of frustration, people bent over backwards to assist a non-threatening senior, injured in a recent fall. He passed through security without a hitch—the woman just ahead reminding him to grab his hat from the conveyor— enjoying the chance to play out the story he'd concocted. A quiet, slow-moving, amiable tourist, a bit caught off guard by the inclement weather, on the way to visit family. Finally secure on the plane, he rested his head on a small pillow supplied by the solicitous flight attendant, pulled the hat over his eyes to close out the possibility of conversation with chatty neighbors, and, medication assisted, sunk straightaway into a restorative nap.

Less than two hours later, he woke to the pilot's announcement of their approach. Somewhat refreshed, but in pain, he paced himself with a half dose of meds. Deplaning, his strategy was simple. A bit more guesswork and a touch of luck. He checked the board for departing flights and, inhabiting his gift for getting lost in a crowd, he sat inert, within easy distance of the gate for the only direct to Houston left among the extensive list of delays and cancellations. He resisted the urge to swallow another pill, controlling his discomfort with even breaths as he munched on a tasteless ham sandwich and sipped the bottled water purchased from a food cart.

~~~

Giving other drivers a wide berth to account for worn tires on side streets untouched by over-taxed road crews, the siblings found a spot in a public lot outside of Eppley. They'd be out of reach long before the car was located.

Emma squeezed Levi's hand. "You look perfect. We've got this."

The last of their weapons grudgingly dropped in a back-alley dumpster along the way, they shouldered their backpacks, hopped an empty shuttle to the terminal and, with the precision born of a decade's practice, relaxed into their roles, becoming different people. Moving through the terminal, they prepared to pass through the normal TSA checkpoint. Qualifying for pre-check status required fingerprinting. They projected ordinary, lone travelers. Carry-on bags only. Laptops out for x-ray.

It was all good until the tech wizard felt the energy of a much more surreal gift he possessed course through him, what Emma called his Third Eye. Honed by years of anxious survival on the streets, Levi had an uncanny capacity for sensing potential threats in their vicinity. He casually rotated and studied the crowd.

The detective he'd seen sprinting from the parking ramp was standing well above the pack, in conversation with someone.

A mass of people parted and Levi locked eyes with the cop's companion.

Anderson.

~~~

Seth hopped to his feet and stored the notes in his back pocket. One foot forward, I saw him propelled back into the chair as if punched by an invisible fist.

"Haaannnk!" I'd become familiar with Seth's emergency signal and followed his outstretched arm down the corridor to the TSA checkpoint. "It's them!"

A toddler staggered at his mother's side, tuned in to the commotion, and matched Seth's shout with a piercing scream.

Seth pushed to his feet, gesturing wildly at the backs of two people making their way through the line. The woman had blond cropped hair. She wore an unremarkable sweater and baggy jeans. The man directly behind her faced us. Buzz cut and skinny jeans, a student on a budget. Eyes wide open, his hair and glasses were different, his face unforgettable.

Levi. Calvin. Whatever his name is.

He laid both hands on the woman's back and whispered into her ear.

Has to be Emma.

They moved through separate body scanners, each grabbing a backpack off the conveyer belt on the other side. In seconds, I lost sight of them amongst the listless flow of human traffic on the path through the concourse.

~~~

Levi tried to ignore the cold sweat that erupted from his pores when he lifted his arms in the body scanner. He gathered his pack, imagined merging with their surroundings and strolled into the amorphous sea of bodies jammed into the concourse.

The siblings re-established the distance necessary to preserve the appearance of strangers, counting gate numbers from their peripheral vision. He resisted the urge to look over his shoulder, replaying the words Emma had so often spoken. "Keep it cool. You and me, Brother."

He knew they spotted the family restroom as one. He felt hope crackle between them. A refuge, to change their appearance one more time. Levi veered left, trusting the lifeline to his sister would bring her to him.

"Hank?" Phil got in front of me.

"It's them." I struggled for words. "The siblings. Into the concourse."

He was back on his phone before I put a whole sentence together. "Dale. The siblings are in the terminal."

I had cloud bursts in my head.

"Steady." The power of his calm drew me back. "Where are they?"

"Concourse A. They made it past security. She has short blond hair. Black backpack. He has a buzz cut and black glasses. Green backpack. Both dressed in blue jeans and light sweaters." He repeated my description to Goodman, then listened. "I'll call it in. Send Victor."

Phil issued orders. "Stay with Seth. Victor is on the way."

Seth sunk in to me, a warmer, drier rerun of the hospital assault. I dropped my jacket and leaned on the wall to steady us.

Phil crossed the walkway to a TSA Agent guarding the exit from the gates, barring re-entry. He showed his badge while he talked. The agent spoke into his mic and, within a few ticks of the clock, an Airport Authority policewoman walked through a side door covered with warning signs. She hustled over to Phil. The combination of TSA, Airport Authority, and a large man in casual clothing advertising the Des Moines PD started to draw attention. The officer took command and stationed them at the far side of the hall, doing her best to shield them from curious onlookers. I couldn't read lips, but it was a fair guess that Phil was giving names and descriptions, using words like dangerous, desperate, and murder.

~~~

Two people, apparent strangers, crossed into Taranis' line of sight. One female. One male. Young. Each with a backpack. Indistinct. Commonplace. They rounded the corner at a well-rehearsed, falsely relaxed pace.

He felt a twinge of pride. He had trained them, after all.

Where was the other team? It didn't matter. He had tracked down his prize pupils. A tolerable bargain.

But, something was off.

Any actor with a keen grasp of character development would have been impressed as the false elder struggled to his feet and triangulated his prey, absently surveying the crowd while he ambled through families and service dogs without haste or urgency.

"Excuse me. Sorry. Thank you." It was easy to spot the cause of the siblings distress. Airport Authority.

Non-verbal cues undiscernable to anyone except the grifters told him the two were synchronized, their familial symbiosis an asset he had exploited in con after con. He saw the subtle shift from fear to hope in the young man's eyes when they targeted a family restroom at the end of a short hallway.

Taranis drifted ahead, into the hallway, slightly hunched over, cane in his left hand. Emma led their approach, ignorant to the absurd notion that their mentor was within reach.

"Sis!" Levi hissed. One footstep too slow, his Third Eye registered a specter his rational mind could not grasp. Emma was shrugging out of her backpack, shelter looming large. Taranis extended his cane to capture her right ankle. She stumbled forward; arms locked into the straps. The stomach-churning crunch of her forehead on hardwood echoed in the closed space. In one fluid motion Taranis rammed the cane into Levi's gut and grabbed his sweater, shoving and pulling the siblings through the door, into the cramped space. Emma crumpled to the floor. Her backpack slid to the wall, her body following in its wake. Levi tripped to the concrete and crab walked to her side. Taranis back sided the door closed and clicked the lock.

"Sis!" Levi shrunk to the corner. Whimpering, he sat, cradling his sister's limp form in his lap, her ghost white, concave face resting on his chest. If not dead, she was dead to his world.

"This is your doing." Taranis shoved aside the visual of two hungry children shoveling food into their mouths in a Denver diner. "Did you believe you could improve on the game I taught you? That I taught you everything I know?"

He leaned in to savor the defeat in Levi's eyes. What he saw was a face transformed.

Burning hate.

Levi twisted his torso and tenderly lowered the head of the only person he had ever loved to the floor. He tossed his knapsack to the side, turned his back to Taranis, and covered her lifeless body with his own.

"You lose," he said. "We win."

The fountain of rage that had fueled Taranis' pursuit of repentance and revenge erupted in the wake of Levi's defiance. He raised the cane above his head. The power of metal against bone and muscle reverberated from his fingers to his own abused skull.

Levi took the blow without a sound.

"I'm here, Sis. Just you and me."

Taranis felt something almost forgotten. Powerlessness. He had been rendered invisible, banished from the siblings' reality.

He wasn't sure how many more times he struck.

There was no time to stop and regulate the electricity rushing through him when he finally dropped the cane. Gathering all he could carry, he readjusted his hat in the mirror, retrieved his weapon and, shielding himself from a final look at the siblings, slipped awkwardly into the hallway.

On an ordinary work day, Taranis would have homed in on unsteady young man with flowing hair who nearly collided with him as he rounded the corner. This was not one of those days. He had to gather himself. He had another flight to catch.

~~~

Seth stared down the hallway.

Get him to safe people, Anderson.

"Seth, let's get you back to your parents." I let go of him. Bending down for my coat, I stumbled against the wall, grasping air where he'd been seconds before.

"Seth!" He was lurching toward the TSA exit.

"Phil!"

I broke into a sprint, closing the distance with shorter strides, but without weeks of sedatives working their way out of my system. Phil reacted in time to see Seth swerve to the left, well out of reach, and launch himself against the grain of bodies, past the TSA Agent, who stepped into my path with remarkable timing. I slammed into him from behind. We sprawled onto the terrazzo, a hairsbreadth from colliding with a stroller and a couple staring at their phones.

The toddler in the stroller clapped, as if we were the evening's entertainment.

A pair of familiar hands lifted me to my feet.

"I see him," Phil said.

"Stop!" The Airport Authority Officer multi-tasked, holding her hand up and checking on the TSA officer.

"Officer Ellis, Seth Oberstreet is in a compromised condition, chasing his kidnappers. This is his therapist, Hank Anderson. We need to catch the boy."

The officer fed the information into her mic. An interminable amount of time went by.

"Sorry, Detective. You cannot go through security in this manner. We have officers in the concourse." She rested her hands on her duty belt. "We're on this. I need you and Mr. Anderson to remain here and…"

I wasn't interested in the rest of her orders.

"Hank!" Phil's voice boomed over the background noise.

"Mr. Anderson! Stop!"

I didn't. Pushing into the crowd, I spotted Seth, face-to-face with another airport cop. Slowing to a walk, I didn't see his partner reach out for me. His thick fingers gripped my shirt. In the instant it took to spin, cuff, and push me to the wall, I caught a glimpse of another officer down the hall to the left, blocking the entrance to a restroom. Two bodies lay immobile, one face up, the other slumped across the first.

Cheek pinned to the wall, the next thing I saw was Phil, Officer Ellis, Victor, and the guy I'd flattened, under the exit, arms crossed. The cop patted me down and stood me up.

"This is probably what Dennis anticipated would happen," I said to the audience that had stopped to stare.

Seth and I were prodded to retrace our steps.

Cordoned off from the crowd, Phil gave the arresting officers enough of Seth's story to convince them handcuffs were a bad idea. His efforts on my behalf were futile. In spite of understanding my good intentions, the Airport Authority officers were busy consulting on the ways I'd defied federal security protocols.

"I'm sorry, Hank. I kind of lost it. All the sudden I wanted to stop the people who tried to hurt me," Seth explained. "I didn't mean to get you in trouble."

"No apology necessary." I was unable to pat him on the shoulder. "I have a gift for getting in trouble without help from anyone."

"How are you doing, Mr. Oberstreet?" Officer Ellis ignored me.

"I'd be better if Hank wasn't in cuffs."

The kid's got spunk.

"I can tell you the suspects are in custody and will be transported to a hospital." She ignored me some more. "My orders are to escort you all to the command center. How about I request a golf cart for transport?"

"That would be nice."

Convinced I was not a risk to flee the country, Officer Ellis uncuffed me before we climbed on the cart.

"These are for real criminals," she said.

"Thank you."

"Don't thank me." We were not going to be friends. "You'll be getting notice of hearing options with regard to your violations. At the very least, this incident could carry significant fines."

"I apologize for making an already chaotic situation worse."

"Sucking up won't help your cause, either. It's my job." She chewed her lower lip.

Second thoughts.

"My report will reflect your intention to assist a seriously at-risk individual. I will avoid phrases like terrorist threat when describing your behavior, with a focus toward well-meaning recklessness and failure to comply with an officer."

The short ride to the Airport Authority offices was enough time to think.

Recklessness and failure to comply. The title of my autobiography. I may need Jill in her lawyer's uniform after-all.

Mom and Dad Oberstreet were in the waiting area of the command center with Goodman. Victor began patiently wading through a credentials check by the desk officer. Delivered dazed and intact, Seth submitted to another binge of hugs from his mother and cast-iron handshakes from his father.

The detectives were invited by a sergeant into the inner sanctum for an update. When they returned, things happened fast. In a remarkable feat of efficiency and cooperation, the airport police, TSA staff, and airline freed the family for boarding.

There was no talk of citing Seth for his excursion. There was no time for an extended goodbye.

Victor stopped on his way out. "Respect for what you did to protect Seth."

"Thanks. One question, Victor."

"Fair enough."

"You're the security chief with, I imagine, a whole team of people. Yet, here you are."

"That's not a question." One corner of his mouth showed the semblance of a smile. "I work for Wyatt. Seth is my friend." His face returned to stone. "I screwed up. Lost him. Twice. It's up to me to get him home."

He noticed Seth motioning me to a corner, offered up a fist bump, and joined the parents.

"I can't focus on all of this at once." Seth took the words out of my mouth. He held up the notes I'd given him. "Today, I'm going home."

Seth imitated Victor, going with a fist bump.

A bunch of guys, and a mom, going their separate ways after an interesting weekend. No big deal.

Seth stood tall and followed Victor into the hallway.

Wyatt hung back.

"I didn't expect to take this up with you until a later date, Hank. You know, job one is getting our son out of here."

"Absolutely."

"I owe you big time. If you've been working by the hour, you are about to become a very rich man." In Wyatt's world, cash was currency for gratitude.

"I'm an honorary police volunteer on this trip, Wyatt." I reached up and slapped him on the shoulder, the way a man's man does. "Your son is an amazing person. If you would favor me with a message when you settle in at home, we'll call it even."

"You are a different kind of guy. Stalwart." He pulled a business card from an ancient wallet, the only visible wardrobe concession to his rugged past. It was blank save a phone number embossed in black. "If I can ever be of service to you, or your family, that's my direct line. I mean it."

I believed him.

A parting question surfaced in me. "Wyatt. What's job two?"

His eyes narrowed and the amiable, rough and ready exterior of a self-made man gave way to the shrouded features of someone Dad would label, the kind of guy you don't want to meet in a dark alley.

He reverted to grateful father. "Hoping justice is served. Those people did a lot of damage."

He wheeled on his bootheels and caught up to Ava, who blew me a parting kiss through the glass.

Stalwart. Might have to put that on a cool, embossed business card.

Office Ellis pointed me to a bench without another word, and went back to work. I was eavesdropping on the conversations of various personnel when the detectives came for me. My talent as a snoop had garnered me the info that the longest day in recent memory became a night of polar opposites. Seth was on his way home, while Emma and Levi were the casualties of an unknown assailant, a piece of irony beyond my comprehension.

I looked at Goodman, defenseless against his next cheap shot.

He shrugged.

"I bring good news, Anderson."

"There's good news?"

"The roads are passible for professional drivers like Phil and myself. You have been released to us. You'll be in your jammies before daybreak. We're going home."

I looked to the big man for confirmation. He placed the fedora on his head, corroborating Goodman's announcement and restoring a degree of order to our world.

"There is security camera footage that covers nearly every step of the siblings' movements through the airport," he said.

"Except the restroom," I guessed.

"Exactly. The police and TSA are reviewing the footage. The Airport Authority Chief has arrived. Dale and I have been questioned."

He looked at his partner.

More relief?

"We gave our version of events. Based on communications above our pay grade, we are excused from further participation in the investigation."

"Catherine?"

"I have consulted my wife and we are cleared for a careful drive home."

"There is one more thing." Goodman said.

"Of course there is."

"You've been put on the Ten Least Wanted List by the Eppley Airport Authority."

Score one for Goodman.

Phil reestablished the plan before the plan taking shape before things went to hell in a handbasket for the fourth time in as many days. We would drop Goodman at his car. Phil would give me a ride back to Des Moines, deposit me home, then reunite with his family. I hoped Goodman's plan included eating his cinnamon roll while having nice thoughts about Lucinda, who had fueled a modest improvement in his general attitude.

I was a bit nervous about venturing into the night so soon after the storm had passed, until one of Dennis' favorite terms intruded into my consciousness.

"Scared backwards, Marlowe." I could hear his speech. "You're more nervous about driving in bad weather with an expert at the wheel than running at a murderer and armed cops in an airport."

I got in the car.

We made it to Goodman's sedan without incident or conversation, none of us with any juice left for banter. The detective cranked his engine, lowered the driver's window in a way only lifers of Midwest weather do, cued up what I recognized as *Kind of Blue* on his Bluetooth, and hit the road.

The loner cop drives off into the distant night, the melancholy of Miles Davis and miles of desolate road his only companions.

Phil and I were looking at two to three hours of highway time, ample opportunity to tweak the narrative of recent events. I started with, "at least all the kids are alive and headed for home." But, even in my current condition, I knew the rationale was weak.

"I'm not always honest, but my intentions are honorable."

"You also tend toward honesty about your dishonesty." He paused. "You're a terrible liar."

"I couldn't even fool Catherine. And she's pure of heart."

"Yes. I suggest we go with the unvarnished truth and deal with the fallout."

"Simple. Elegant."

He rested his hat on the dashboard, turned the key, and we followed his partner across the Iowa state line, into the night. Our headlights burned a narrow corridor, Phil taking us through the hills that gave Council Bluffs gets its name with his limited understanding of the attack on the sibling outlaws.

"They were lost in the crowd, and then what?"

"They went into a family restroom, probably to make additional changes in their appearance, get back onto the streets, and disappear into the city." The dashboard lights reflected his disbelief. "These people can…could…really think on their feet. There are no details on who assaulted them while the airport police were closing in. No one saw it."

We lapsed into silence. My friend needed to concentrate on the drive home.

In a land of experienced bad weather drivers, interstate highways, on nights like these, were primarily built for the unsuspecting and overconfident. The DOT was fighting the good fight, but a northwesterly wind refused to quit. Patches of ice, ground into the pavement, lay in wait beyond our sight lines. I soon lost count of the number of solitary pickup trucks, cars, and 4-wheel drive SUVs—they are better at gathering speed in bad weather but spin out on ice like every other vehicle—abandoned on the shoulder, hazard lights blinking, or nose down in a ditch. Watching

Phil give space to the flashing lights of wreckers and patrol cruisers drew my thoughts to the major and Goodman the Elder.

Closing in on the Atlantic exit, traffic slowed to the pace of rush hour in Des Moines. Phil piloted us past an active multi-car crash, set off by a jackknifed tractor trailer. Mutual antagonism aside, I was glad none of the cars were driven by our Goodman. We were waved through by the patrol on site, both of us relieved to find people sitting upright, keeping warm in the backseats of the cruisers, no ambulances on the scene.

On the other side of the pileup, Phil handed me a small cache of CDs. I dropped Junip into the player, the band's clash of melancholy and optimism a fitting soundtrack for our path through the flatlands.

SUNDAY MORNING

By the time we reached the suburbs the storm had pressed on to take up residence in Chicago. The radio's prediction of dry, overcast skies was a perfect match for the prevailing mood in the car. Street lights reflected off the untended sidewalks of my neighborhood. It seemed as if we had been away for weeks on an elusive quest for some fundamental truth. I had too many miles on my moral compass to name what it was.

Phil parked in the driveway. "I apologize for exposing you to all of this."

I gave him the two-fisted handshake I save for special people. "Well, I guess we kept an eye on each other."

"Which I will omit in my explanation to Catherine."

"The better part of valor."

I groaned, trading the warmth of the car for the crisp humidity. Fetching my bag from the back seat, I fingered the jacket. "I'm going to keep this terrific rain parka as payment for services." We both tried to smile. "I'd appreciate any updates you can give me."

"I'll do what I can. The same from you." He knew I'd stay apprised of Seth's recovery.

I gave a final salute as his headlights crossed over me.

Standing alone, I realized I had no quiet way to get into my house. No remote. No keys. Just the sound of the garage door creaking loudly if I entered the secret code.

The motion detector on the porch light kicked on when Dad opened the front door, flannel PJs, coffee mug in one hand, cane under his arm.

"Come in out of the cold, Son." He lifted the mug in my direction. "Thought you might find your way home early. How about a bite to eat?"

I pointed at the cane. "You have a new accessory."

"Come inside. We'll talk."

Dad sat at the counter while I dug into a warmed-up stack of leftover blueberry pancakes. Not wanting to fence with my exhaustion, I did the unthinkable and drank decaf.

"How's Haley?" I wanted to see my daughter as soon as possible.

"Amazing. We had a fine time. Mostly with her friend, Kelli. My favorites got postponed due to weather."

"The zoo. The art museum. The Farmer's Market," I said. The man loved family, AA, cheeseburgers, and produce. In that order.

"Right. We cooked. She convinced me to try a soy burger." He frowned. "They took turns hammering me into submission on the chess board. I dropped them off at Gail's last night to avoid disruption."

And.

"Gail wants you to give her a call before you talk to Haley, in case there's any more craziness to report. Her words, not mine."

"I will and there is. After a few hours of sleep."

"Sounds like a good idea." He stood to gather my dish, stopping to lean against the stove.

"What is it Dad?" He wasn't giving the facts up easily, but ask a straight question, I could expect a straight answer.

"I meant to tell you as soon as I got here, but you needed to get on the road to help Phillip."

I let him have that one.

"I had a fall." The last time I'd seen him this forlorn was the day he admitted himself for alcoholism treatment. "I came strolling in after they mopped the floor at closing time. Wasn't paying attention. The doc says it's a meniscus tear. I won't need surgery if I take it easy. Ice. Elevation. Plenty of rest." He looked at the cane like it was his enemy. "Plus, use this contraption."

I had to rest my elbows on the counter, head in my hands. "You're not dying."

"Oh my." He eased onto the stool next to me. "No. No. But I have some tough decisions to make."

"Decisions?" I was too tired to keep up.

"I've had an offer to buy the restaurant." His announcement lacked enthusiasm. "It's a good offer."

"Luis can run the restaurant while you're rehabbing." I stopped myself. "Sorry. Let's chalk up my uninvited attempt to fix your problem to a lack of sleep."

"The offer is from Luis."

He didn't need to tell me what this meant. Luis Morales had taken over more responsibility as restaurant manager in the past several years. He knew every part of the business. He was the best cook, bar none, that had ever landed in Mom and Dad's kitchen. Luis and his wife, Rosa, had spoken to my father many times about their dream of owning a business, as they carved out a Midwestern life for themselves and their two sons in a part of the country not currently famous for cultural diversity. Now, there was an offer for Luis to step into Dad's shoes.

"It's not about money."

"No. I love the business. It's the people and the years."

I refilled our decaf.

"And your mom."

There it is.

We sat and let memories of her fill the room.

"Dean said he'd stay on as the new manager, and no offense to you, I can't think of anyone who would take better care of your mom and my life's work than Luis and Rosa."

"Agreed. But, then what?"

"Excellent question. I sit around, rehab my knee? Learn to care about crabgrass?"

I pictured my recent session with Alicia. "Not likely."

"But this is the wrong time to go into all of this." He clipped the end of his sentence. "You're tapped out. We'll talk more when we're rested."

"When you're right, you're right." I was more than ready for the comfort of my loft. "How about we catch up with those dishes after some down time."

"Good idea."

Shuffling toward my cocoon on the first landing, a grain of irritation sifted through my malaise. The hard-fought changes in our relationship also demanded directness from me.

"Hey, Dad. You faked your way through the injury pretty well to get me out the door with Goodman. Not cool. It was way beyond scary wondering what you were going to tell me when I got home."

He limped out of the kitchen. "Point taken."

"Where was the cane?"

It was his turn to look sheepish. "I kept it in the car to downplay the seriousness of what happened." He looked straight at me, cutting through his guilt. "I called my AA sponsor and he reminded me that's not how I do things anymore. I owe you an amends. I'm sorry, Son."

"All is forgiven. I still have some work to do in the truth telling department myself. One more thing. You know you could move up here with me. To recuperate. Or to stay."

"You definitely need a lot of rest."

"Haley would be thrilled. So would I. Think about it."

"I will." He tapped his heart. "No matter what I decide, I am grateful for the offer. Now, how about we shut this party down before we fall asleep standing up."

"Good idea." I started and stopped one more time. "Oh yeah. I forgot. Lucinda from Omaha says hi."

He grew a smile. "Isn't she a gem." He flexed to a fake frown. "I didn't see you bring a takeout box into the house. You men must have eaten all of the blackberry rhubarb pie."

"Goodnight, Dad."

"Good to have you home, Son."

Leaning into the cane, he shuffled toward the guest bedroom on the first floor. I moaned my way up the stairs, traded my clothes for washed-out sweats, and dropped into bed. My skin ached. My hair hurt. The inside of my head felt like a hand full of sputtering sparklers.

I started counting loved ones.

Haley. Dad. Dennis. Belinda. Phil. Gail. Jerry. Catherine. Jill.

THE MIGHTY SHALL FALL

I woke to the sound of the doorbell and a subdued greeting to the ringer of the bell, after very little sleep. I rested my hand on the indentation left by the woman who successfully kept me awake until the wee hours.

"How are you feeling?" Jill had asked last night. Again.

Weeks later, I could not fully describe the bruise to my spirit that followed me into sleep each night and greeted me every morning, a wound born of the destruction of four more tragically misspent lives. People had died. Not in my house, not this time. Not by my hand, or even within my line of sight. They had all been criminals, violent criminals.

These were the facts. They provided little consolation.

I had divined the answer to the question that plagued me from the beginning of this mess. How did Seth end up in my office?

"Lawrence told me you would give me something to help me feel better." Seth's exact words at the end of our first session.

The Scholars of Calm thought I could prescribe him medication. A more common mistake about various professions that start with the letters—psych—than one might think.

I hadn't told anyone. Knowing the truth can be critical, or irrelevant.

Jill had been both moved and shocked by my willingness to place myself between Seth and the siblings. She repeatedly stressed that I had fulfilled my commitment to Seth, with the bonus payoffs of keeping my foolish promise to Catherine, standing in support of Phil, and surviving a thorny partnership with Detective Dale.

My Al-Anon sponsor suggested I required further work on my desire to control more of life than was humanly possible, proving I wasn't the only person on the planet with an excellent grasp of the obvious.

Dennis had been a prince, bringing me a regular flow of listening ear and apple fritters. He let me know he had tabled all planned lectures about my behavior, given his belief that anything he'd offer was already taking up space in my head.

"I will say, that if asked by Belinda or Gail, I intend to completely deny my next statement," he told me. "Jerry and I think the way you blew through TSA security to protect Seth was totally bad-ass."

Belinda blessed me by taking a vacation from making coffee. "I'm so happy you and the detectives found those children, you wonderful, crazy man," became her standard greeting. She even dropped donuts off at the police station. "Don't be thinking I like Detective Goodman. But, he did help you find the children."

I liked it when she described him as my helper.

It was all good medicine. But it didn't erase several additional truths. Seth had, himself, escaped The Scholars. The other students were released by desperate people as the scam began circling the drain. The young man who pointed the gun in our direction was much more proficient at subterfuge than firearms. And, compliment from Dennis and Jerry aside, I knew in retrospect that chasing Seth into the concourse could have resulted in far worse consequences than whatever fines and restrictions were coming my way.

In the mystery novels I devoured as a youth, the heroes and anti-heroes often beat overwhelming odds to solve the crime.

The detectives and I weren't heroes. We'd been persistent. And lucky.

"I can't hear what's in your head, Anderson," Jill had reminded me.

"Sorry. My thoughts are all over the place. They're not scar tissue. Yet. I am most definitely better with you here."

After we made love, the remaining scent of eucalyptus on her skin lulled me to sleep.

Doorbell, Anderson. Visitor.

I pulled myself back, certain it was healthier to greet my guest than stay stuck in my head. I leveraged the residual compassion from Jill, slipped into jeans and a black thermal shirt, and made my way down to the living room. The shades on the glass French doors to the patio were open to an unexpected sun shining on the snow that arrived overnight.

The guest was Phil. Jill was showing off her recently acquired skill for brewing drinkable coffee. The detective and I hadn't seen much of one another since Omaha. I assumed he was hard at work on his marital relationship, and paying penance on the job. He was decked out in a gold-on-purple track suit, absent the fedora. He looked well rested. I imagined he'd been up at dawn jogging or lifting cars by the bumper.

My former attorney and the detective had a choppy backstory, based on the necessary roles they played during the first mess in the fall. No worries. Both saw themselves as my advocate and came to respect the other as a formidable opponent. Now, both were members of my inner circle.

"Two of my favorite people sharing a cup of joe...brew...mud...java...perk...ink."

I've been studying.

Jill, sitting resplendent in Drake U casual, rolled her eyes. She pointed at the mug on the end table. "Extra cream."

I took a grateful sip and feigned astonishment.

"Don't get used to it, Anderson." She grinned.

"Your smile could reheat a cuppa go-juice."

A bigger grin.

She likes me.

Phil maintained radio silence. If he'd been surprised by the official greeter to his unannounced visit on a Sunday morning, his face gave nothing away.

"Good morning." Dad made his appearance from the back bedroom with a slight limp, cane free, fully groomed, his full head of gray hair combed neatly. "Is this a private party, or can an old man join you?"

"It's good to see you, Mr. Anderson." Phil stood. "Please join us."

"Good to see you, too, Detective. Remember, J.R. to my friends." His eyes landed on Jill. "Seeing you is a lovely way to start the day, young lady." He patted her arm. "I could get used to this."

I was pretty sure Jill would punch any other guy who addressed her in that manner.

"Can I get you a cup of coffee, J.R.?"

"No. No," he insisted. "A brisk, but careful, walk to the kitchen gets my engine started."

Off he went.

"Dry run," I explained. "Dad's recovering from a knee injury. No surgery if he takes it slow. He might sell the restaurant and move in with me. I got him to agree to stay for a spell, to see how we'd do as roommates."

Only a skilled psychotherapist would notice Phil's face showed a spark of approval.

"What brings you my way on a church day, other than a quality cup of battery acid?"

"We went wild. Did Saturday evening church to shake things up."

Wow. Religious humor.

"I wanted to give you a face-to-face update on the Oberstreet situation."

"How is the young man?" Dad had his cup.

"From what both Hank and I hear he's doing quite well. According to our reports, all of the students are receiving ongoing counseling." He took a sip. "This is about the status of the criminals."

"It's been on our minds." Jill shot me a look.

And keeping us awake at night.

Phil shook his head. "The brother, who insists on others continuing to call him Levi, not his given name of Calvin, has been held in hospital detention since his arrest. He sustained serious injuries, but will have a full recovery.

The charges against him are extensive. Without any promise of consideration, he offered to cooperate with the federal authorities."

"Federal authorities?" I was out of my legal depth.

Jill jumped in. "Taking Seth and his buddies across state lines under false pretenses. Attempted kidnapping. Attempted murder. Accessory to murder. Bank and other financial fraud." Attorney Bennett ticked off what sounded like an abbreviated introduction to a multitude of offenses. "I'm guessing several agencies are falling all over themselves trying to get to the front of the line on this one."

"There is some jostling for position," said Phil. "The Des Moines Police Department is not at the top of the heap."

I circled back. "Why is Levi being so cooperative?"

"His sister. Emma. Levi says the assault came from Taranis. They were caught off guard by a disguise he had not used before."

"Emma?"

"Yes. He won't answer to Calvin and he won't call his sister Debra."

Attempts to detach from trauma covers a lot of ground.

"She sustained a traumatic brain injury from the attack and will spend the rest of her life under constant care," Phil said. "Partial paralysis. Seizures. Slurred speech. She has no memory of the crimes she committed."

"She'll be declared unfit to stand trial," Jill added.

My gut butterfly flapped in uncertain rhythm.

Sociopaths? Psychopaths? Dissociation? Brain injury.

I could not diagnose people I had never met. Without question, though, the siblings' singular loyalty to one another had been refined by their life together on the streets. In the end, others would carry the burden of the suffering caused by and laid upon the young murderess and her brother. I revisited a depth of sadness for the children raised by the mental health and social services systems. Many show remarkable resilience under the care of talented, committed, compassionate caregivers. Many falter, caught in a web of revolving doors and substandard care.

"Levi's revenge."

"Yes," Phil said. "First of all, he confirms that The Scholars of Calm was nothing more than a cover for conning the students, Seth in particular, out of as much money as they could get their hands on. They studied and used the indoctrination methods of cults, but the entire operation was a scam. He has also shared a thorough mental dossier of the man they knew as Taranis. Aliases on passports and credit cards. Favorite false identities, minus the one he used in the assault. Multiple residences. Levi could see or hear the information once and remember the details."

"Eidetic memory plus, no honor among thieves," Dad said.

"Exactly," Phil said. "One more thing. We now know that Taranis' given name is Mick C. Richards. Found written on the inside of an old paperback book hidden in a safe."

"Safe?"

"Levi was vague with the interviewers on this point, J.R. The feds believe there was some kind of coup by the siblings, setting off the attack at the airport."

"Taranis. Richards. Calvin. Levi. Hard to follow," Dad said.

"That was the idea. Other than the arrest of Musslewhite and Braxton, and Musslewhite's history of drug use, these people escaped notice for years. After we finished, as Dale says, chasing our tails around the countryside, we followed the trail of their leader's name. He has no criminal record, adult or juvenile. He's a native of Missouri. His parents are deceased. His older brother is career army. They haven't been in contact for more than ten years."

A past brief and unpleasant interaction with the DEA told me what came next.

"Which is the end of our investigation. People at the federal level are in charge now and we won't be party to their additional interviews with Levi. Suffice to say, they will be scouring the northern hemisphere for Richards."

He stood to leave.

Still not big on casual conversation.

"Thanks for catching us up, Phil," I said.

"The least I could do. Thanks for the coffee, Jill. I'm past due at home, with a large box of fresh pastries." He closed the space and engulfed Dad's hand. "Wonderful to see you, J.R. Best wishes on whatever decisions you make." He pointed to Dad's knee. "Take it easy on that injured wheel."

"Will do, Phil."

"One more thing." Jill wasn't done.

"Certainly."

"Hank was almost killed on his bicycle. Who and why?"

"A part of Levi's story that doesn't quite hold up. He says he blamed you for throwing a wrench into their scheme and decided to do a hit-and-run. The Scholars of Calm had the SUV hidden in the woods, which is probably true. He claims to have tracked down your address online, followed you to the bike trail, and waited for you to ride back onto the street."

"You don't believe him," I said.

"He had already left the camp, another piece of the puzzle we don't understand. But, Emma was the premeditated killer. We believe she poisoned Musslewhite and set Braxton up for the fall. We're sure she murdered

Braxton. Toxicology tells us the soda she tried to give Seth at the hotel was spiked with a powerful dose of sedatives."

"I've been imagining what she was planning next for him," I said.

"Whatever it was, she failed." Jill laid her hand on my knee. "But Levi is the one who shot at Hank."

"Their attack at the hospital was a last-ditch effort to grab Seth and force him to transfer his money to off-shore bank accounts held by Taranis, accounts that Levi had already hacked. Levi maintains he panicked when Hank and Seth ran."

We were about to enter the territory of broad speculation, something I knew Phil preferred to avoid.

"Which may or may not be true," he said. "It is true that he's a follower with a ten-year criminal history whose only attachment in life is his sister, so I'm not surprised his story has holes in it. The feds may not be able to fill all the holes. What matters is what you said, Jill. Emma and Levi failed and are in custody."

"Thank you, Phil. Give my best to Catherine."

"Will do, Jill." He hunched a shoulder toward the entryway. "A private moment, Hank?"

"I'll walk you out."

~~~

We stood side-by-side on the front stoop, staring into the street, our breath blowing smoke rings in the chill. Darts of sun bounced off the snow.

"I seldom assume," he began. "Today, I'll make an exception. This tragedy has been added to the heavy weight you still carry from the deaths during what you and Dennis call the mess in the fall."

Yes.

"I will not pretend to know how you will find relief from those burdens, or who you will allow to lift them from you. I simply trust that you will do all that is possible. And I will offer this." He stepped onto the walkway to balance our height differential. "I am not an easy man to know. With rare exception, I keep to myself." He turned to me. "But you already know these things."

Yes.

"You are not a replacement for Matthew. You are one of my people. You risked a great deal for me. Again. You risked a great deal for my family. Again. I will not forget. God bless you, my friend."

He covered the distance to his car in a few steps. I watched him leave, transformed from champion of the young and vulnerable to family food delivery guy.

I crouched down and cupped a handful of melting snow. On my heels, I packed a perfect snowball and threw it at the trunk of the closest tree. The chill in my hand was a pleasant contrast to the heat in my heart. I raised my eyes to whoever or whatever might be listening.

"Bless you too, pal."

Getting into Mexico had been easy. He was on standby and took the first open seat to Dallas.

By the time he walked across the border, the bump on his head had receded into a constant, dull ache. An upgraded bamboo walking stick was his new favorite prop. He was no longer an elderly gentleman in need of assistance. He was a cheerful vacationer on his way to Cancun; a man who invested well from income supplied by an accident of uncertain detail, suffering from occasional migraines and a permanent hitch in his step.

Staying in Mexico was more complex, but doable. His passport allowed him six months on a visitor's permit. He had the contacts necessary to obtain a visa through unofficial channels, and enough time and money to find a hacker to get through the walls set up by Levi, to re-coop another portion of his savings.

He allowed the surge of fire in his belly to float into the cloudless sky. Not the mother lode he had planned on, but he'd been forced to move fast.

In the meantime, he was playing the part of the single tourist, sipping potent umbrella cocktails and taking in the vastness of the waves washing up sand from everywhere, chasing sandpipers and kids from the water's edge.

Kids. That's all they were when he found them. Not the way he wanted it to end. Emma. Unnecessarily lost to her grandiosity and greed. Levi. A brilliant sheep, herded in whatever direction his sister demanded. Carlos and Kenton? Perhaps he would know more of their whereabouts when he accessed his accounts and learned what had been harvested by the traitors.

He was, once again, operating solo. His life had come full circle.

His eyes wandered the sunburned masses, landing on three scant bikinis. Even tans. Flat stomachs. Well past the age of students on holiday. Single, married, or divorced. He didn't care. He knew they were looking for an interesting story to take home from vacation. One they would only share among themselves. One kept secret when they discovered their credit cards had been compromised.

He'd look good to them. A guy who knew his way around a gym. Dark hair. Mirrored sunglasses suggesting a touch of danger. He'd come up with a more interesting lie to explain his limp. A conversation starter.

Adjusting the loose white trousers that covered his fake injury, the con man turned pick-up artist was reaching for his stick when a silhouette glided into his path, a human solar eclipse.

"Excuse me, friend. You're obstructing an exceptional view."

"Mr. Richards."

Hearing the name he had almost forgotten lodged a stone in his chest.

The thief shaded his eyes with a level hand, revealing nothing but scornful humor. The youthful, athletic man before him was dressed impeccably in a beige linen shirt and shorts combo with multi-colored running shoes.

"I'm afraid you have me confused with someone else."

"I'm sure I haven't." No facial expression, no emotion in a voice carrying a twinge of a Latin accent he didn't recognize. "My name is Victor and I need you to come with me."

Taranis shook his head. "No," he said. "What I will do is insist the bartender call security."

Before he could stand, a hand the size of a hot pan holder landed easily on his shoulder from behind, holding him in the lounge chair.

"That won't be necessary." Victor pointed over the thief's shoulder, to the person attached to the hand. "I've taken it upon myself to bring the Corporal with me. The Corporal is with the Policìa Federal and has agreed to accompany us. He has already spoken with the bartender."

The grifter's thoughts raced ahead. Engage the mark. "Victor. How about I buy you and the officer a drink. We can discuss this mistake."

"Arrangements have been made." Victor replied as if he hadn't heard him speak. "You won't be needing this." Victor took the cane and handed it to the policeman.

"I've got money, gentlemen." He scanned the walkway from the beach to his bungalow.

Victor followed his eyes. "Everything in your room has been taken care of. It's time to go."

Laptop. Bank codes. Cash. Credit cards. Passports and IDs. They had it all.

When the hand prodded him from the beach chair he saw it was attached to a man with oversized parts bonded to his torso. Everything on the Mexican policeman was large: head, biceps, chest. Everything except his gut, which looked like a flat-iron plate. A serious looking sidearm rested in the holster below his bulletproof vest. The cop appeared sleepy, but the thief knew it was an act.

Richards realized he was the only one sweating profusely. "Two questions, if I may."

"I'll answer if I can."

"Why have you come for me?"

"This time you hurt people equipped to fight back."

"How did you find me?"

"It was a serious mistake to harm the sister of a criminal who holds such intimate knowledge of your methods." The racket of children and surf retreated while Victor further considered his answer. "After you harmed the son of people who have considerable resources and know many well-placed individuals."

Through the cloud of defeat, the con man processed the information. Levi was alive and the rich kid's family had the resources to reach all the way into Mexico. He was genuinely impressed.

Casting an eye over the spectacular landscape one last time, he regained a measure of calm. "If you will permit me, one final question."

Victor waited.

"Will you please kill me quickly?"

The policeman spoke for the first time as he steered Taranis away from the beach.

"There will be no killing today, Mr. Richards. The authorities look forward to meeting with you when you cross back into the United States."

Victor led the way up the sand-sprinkled footpath. The policeman kept a loose grip on Taranis' elbow. No cuffs were necessary.

An unmarked Jeep with full privacy glass sat in the circle drive of the resort, stark in contrast to the exotic multi-colored flower beds and garish fountain welcoming foreign guests. Victor occupied the front passenger seat next to the driver, an officer of lower rank. The corporal filled half of the back seat after depositing Taranis behind the driver. The click of the door locks ended all conversation.

It was more than an hour's silent drive to the airport. They rode at a steady and cautious speed through the mayhem of taxis, trucks, luxury and barely functioning cars, and assorted two-wheeled vehicles belching carbon into the city.

A sunburned, heavily armed man in a green camo uniform opened the locked gate at a secluded entrance to the small airfield. No security. No customs. Victor came around and ushered Richards from the back seat. The driver unloaded the bags from the hatchback and crossed the tarmac, placing them in the aft compartment of a sleek gray on red Cirrus Vision jet. The corporal shook hands with Victor and stood watch.

From the beach to the runway, Taranis struggled to see the flaw in the practices he had cultivated over so many years. It came to him on the stairs leading into the cabin of the plane.

He stopped to enlighten his captor. "I gave them too much leash. And I underestimated them."

Victor followed. "No. You overestimated yourself."

~~~

I decided it was a good day to cook.

Jill offered to assist with a late breakfast. Dad relaxed on the sofa, sipping orange juice. I cued up Fleet Foxes on vinyl and joined her in the kitchen.

"Good tunes." Dad's tastes ran from The Four Tops and The Everly Brothers—who spent much of their childhood in Iowa—to Bela Fleck and Brandi Carlisle. Eclectic.

"Which reminds me, Dad. Slippery When Wet is in town between shows. I invited James for Liu's Chinese carryout later this week."

"It'll be good to catch up with him on the latest technology." J.R. and James had become pals during the first mess in the fall. "What time will Haley be here?"

"Gail left a message. They're on the way."

"Family. Good music. First-class accommodations." He held his glass up in a toast. "I could get used to this."

"I hope so."

"As a soon to be retired restauranteur, I would also say the two of you work well together."

Jill bumped me with her elbow. "The man is too smooth. Maybe I picked the wrong Anderson."

The front door lock jiggled. Haley made her entrance, tossing her parka at the coat tree and kicking off the black on gold U of Iowa running shoes of her mother's alma mater.

"Mom says hi to everybody." She gave hugs all around. "I'm hungry."

"It's ready to go," Jill said. "Let's eat."

In keeping with the Anderson credo that a quality meal should require more time to eat than cook, we were seated on kitchen stools, collectively working on seconds of J.R.'s famous home baked sourdough toast when the doorbell rang for the second time this morning.

"I got it." Haley jetted for the door before anyone else moved a muscle. She zoomed back to the kitchen with a 10x8 cardboard box in hand. "Delivery guy. It was on the porch. Addressed to you, Dad." She set it on the counter.

My infamous curiosity was piqued and I reached for a kitchen knife to cut the tape. There was a handwritten note sitting on top of the bubble wrap:

Dear Hank,

It's been a challenging time. I'm following through on your recommendations and am definitely on the mend. Thanks for reviewing everything with my therapist, some of the details are still foggy. She says I'm recovering from PTSD. I'll return to school for the spring semester. We'll continue our work when I'm home for breaks.

I have a new game in development. I wanted to give you an early look at the concept. Please make sure to read the blurb.

Hope you are doing well,
Seth
P.S. Mom and Dad say hi.

I set the note aside and pulled a glossy video case from the wrapping.

PRE-RELEASE COVER: NOT FOR SALE
THE MIGHTY SHALL FALL

The title on the case was splashed with polished crimson, dripping in progressively paler droplets over the image of a ghost-white youth with flowing ebony hair, clad head to toe in forest green leather and standing upright on a rocket-powered catamaran racing through a squall of rain and knife-like cones of hail. In one hand he gripped the till, in the other he wielded a thick, bound book shooting beams of radiant light to part the gale and guide his way. A distant, misty background held the stark images of a band of warriors—all shapes, sizes, genders, and colors—dressed in a mashup of knights of medieval times armor and futuristic space gear.

I turned the case over and read the description:

Deandro Styrhaven has been adrift in the Sea of Reprisal, racing against time, since the Flood of Fools. It's been four lexeons since the boy has seen dry land.

Under the veil of the storm he created, The Betrayer kidnapped Styrhaven's originators and destroyed his village, the demon's army of synthetic Kharons laying waste to the entire province of Vrland, in search of the boy's trail. If not for the Stories of Light, Deandro would have perished.

The Betrayer's power grows with each feast of sentient beings. But the wraith will not truly be sated until he devours young Styrhaven in the presence of the Ancestors, the only method by which one can break, and steal, his bond to the Stories. Half human, half enchanted one, born of the ancients, Deandro knows he must find the Narrow Pathway, make his way to the four remaining Warriors of the Tempest, and fulfill the Prophecy of the Fifth.

Constanze. Alden. Severo. Reinier.

The Keepers of Hope.

Deandro cannot predict all that lies ahead. Of this he is certain. It is his destiny to complete the Circle of Vrland. Or die.

"What is it, Son?"

"A video game." I tapped the blurb. "And a new form of trauma healing."

I slid the case in Dad's direction. Jill and Haley read over his shoulder.

"Is this from somebody you helped, Dad?"

"I can't say."

"Cool. Which one are you?"

"It's a game, kiddo."

"We'll see." Cover in hand, the family comet sped out of the kitchen.

About the time we'd finished cleanup, she strolled back in with a self-satisfied expression.

"Got it, Dad."

"Got what?"

She held up the box. "Constanze has Latin roots meaning steadfast. That's the awesome major I overheard you telling Jill about."

"Overheard?"

She ignored me.

"Alden means wise friend. Has to be Uncle Phil." Haley collected friends with a flair inherited from her grandpa. She had adopted Phil along the way and seemed to be well on her way to adding Jill to her merry band.

"Of course, Severo means stern." She ticked off names with her fingers. "Uncle Dennis, Aunt Belinda, or that serious grump, Detective Goodman." She shook her head. "Too many choices."

The whole room laughed.

"Which leaves us with Reinier." Haley drum rolled on the countertop with her fingertips. "Counselor Warrior." She pointed at the smallest figure in the background. "That's you."

~~~

I sat alone, drawn in by the embers in the fireplace and the warmth that filled our house. Jill was upstairs at my desk, prepping for an early morning meeting. Last month, she'd offered to suit up and take on the government's response to what Dennis was calling, The Mess at Eppley. A hefty fine and one-year on the federal no-fly list was the best we could do.

The penalties seemed fair to me.

Haley had retreated to her bedroom to finish tomorrow's homework. After breakfast, she asked me to buy her a copy of The Mighty Shall Fall when it was released. Not to play. To show off to her friends.

Dad was absorbed in adding character to the guest room with his collection of vintage root beer mugs and more photos of mom. Each time we made an AA and Al-Anon road trip home, he returned to Des Moines with a few more tangible memories. Next up he had an appointment with his attorney, to prepare paperwork for the sale of the restaurant to Luis and Rosa.

Over coffee, a friend recently used a word to describe her best life in the midst of loss and love, illness and health, stress and the wonder of each day.

Contentment.

Take it in while it lasts, Anderson.

I smiled and closed my eyes.

ACKNOWLEDGEMENTS

Although the Hank Anderson series is fiction, I write from a desire to provide readers with a certain amount of food for thought (see how I played off of Hank's childhood in the restaurant business). If you are entertained by my novels, I am overjoyed. If you find other levels of meaning and value within the suspense and attempts at humor, all the better.

Much love and gratitude to my daughter, Aimee, who found time in her already fast-moving schedule to become both an early reader and the copy editor for The Mighty Shall Fall. You promised a rigorous review and you delivered!

Appreciation and love to my wife, DiAnne, and my son, Nathan, my other go-to early readers. Without your efforts, plot holes would loom large and I would wonder if the initial draft was interesting to anyone other than myself.

Another round of thanks to my friend and the editor of *Overnight Delivery*, Mary, who agreed to be an early reader and who, caught up in skill and kindness, once again helped me write a better book.

Appreciation to Mary and Tony for their assistance with cover selection.

Thanks to my sister, Lisa, my brother, Kevin, my nephew, Josh, and the many friends, family members, and colleagues who have encouraged me in my efforts to move from nonfiction, mental health author to the creation of Hank Anderson and his family.

Thanks to Helen Claire Gould and Colin Brett of Fiction Fix Online for providing the platform for indie and self-published authors to reach an international audience through live streamed readings during the height of the pandemic. The feedback is always positive and encouraging. It's been great fun!

Thanks to Mark, owner of Spine Bookstore & Café in St. Louis, MO for his support of indie and self-published authors.

My thanks to those professionals I have researched and interacted with in my own career over many years: Law enforcement, attorneys, restaurant owners, video game aficionados, airport staff, and others. I appreciate your grace in my efforts to blend a degree of authenticity with the fiction of *The Mighty Shall Fall*.

AN EXCERPT FROM THE NEXT HANK ANDERSON NOVEL!

THE LAST STEP

The fear drove his imagination. His rational mind knew the Mona Lisa Effect was a myth. Still, it felt like the eyes of the yeoman standing tall on the label of the unopened bottle of Beefeater's London gin followed him from the middle of the lop-sided table to every corner of the room.

He tried to pretend it wasn't there, fully aware he was the man who laid down the cash and walked the booze out the door of the liquor store.

Staring at the blank phone screen, he told himself he should have called for help. Instead, he did the last thing anyone would have expected of him at this stage of his life. He ran away from home.

He'd gone down his list of rationalizations. He couldn't put Jerry or Belinda in danger. Marlowe and his dad were in the middle of a special day. His sponsor worked a good program, but he was a carpenter with little kids, not a private investigator.

All of them lame.

It wasn't difficult to hide out. He was a past master. His skills of avoidance and escape had been honed decades ago, necessary for the survival of the fittest mayhem of meth he was born into. It was a simple matter of dusting off dormant skills from the shadows of his past.

But in today's world, there were complications. Responsibilities. Friends. Clients. The love of his life.

Then there was the integrity thing he lectured others on day in and day out.

A power surge of failure coursed through his body in a way he had not experienced since the day he stood on the porch of the half-way house. Seventeen years ago he had re-entered the normie world, whatever the hell that was. He'd been almost paralyzed by the belief he had burned all of his bridges with the people he loved.

He'd been wrong. After treatment, the fog cleared enough for him to see how many were still waiting for him.

Then he met Jerry. And Marlowe. And Belinda. Haley. Gail. Phil.

Dammit.

He stalked the room, a few short steps away from immobilized by the possibility he could lose the people, old and new, who helped him craft a new life. Maybe he was wrong. Again.

He closed his eyes and whispered Step 1 into the chill: "We admitted we were powerless over alcohol and that our lives had become unmanageable." He let the words seep back into his marrow.

He opened his eyes and crossed the room, picked the yeoman up by the neck, and walked to a weather-beaten door barely attached to its battered frame. The rusted hinges screamed when he kicked the door open. With the grace of the ex-frisbee fanatic, he lofted the fifth of his personal poison into the center of a dumpster in the middle of the trash strewn asphalt lot behind the abandoned house. His view of the flawless arc was hindered by darts of interstate headlights over the eastern rise. The echo of shattered glass and faint odor of high-end alcohol floated on the brittle night wind, a rush of dangerous pleasure.

He looked up. Four strobe-like stars flickered through his misery.

"It's a start."

He made a half-hearted attempt to secure the long-lost door, rolled his mummy bag onto the bargain bin cot and surveyed the remains of his dilapidated childhood home, abandoned years ago, its decay a testimony to the violent collapse of his parents' marriage. He zipped his jacket, pulled a stocking cap over his ears, and burrowed into the cocoon, the rigid crossbar in perfect line with the small of his back.

"Practice what you preach. Make the call." He checked his dwindling battery. The phone was topped out with unreturned text and voice messages. His shame shivered through the cold weather gear.

He shut it down. The phone, not the shame.

"Tomorrow. Progress, not perfection." Out loud, his use of a favorite Twelve Step slogan took the form of an excuse, not a commitment.

Unable to find any comfort, physical or otherwise, he managed a feeble version of his well-known sardonic grin. Few would believe he had spent even one night in such crude lodging in the course of his life.

In truth, few people knew his entire story.

The rhythmic whoosh of constant traffic on the two-lane beyond the blighted hideaway infiltrated his efforts at sleep. An outdated carbon boot print muscle car tore down the road. Its modified muffler announced every acceleration. But it was his mind on a merry-go-round of memories about this tainted place mingling with a sense of helplessness that provided all the noise necessary to beat away his exhaustion.

"What does this dirtbag want from me?" He could not fathom the purpose of the burner phone he'd received.

In the meantime, Marlowe's excitable voice, full of questions, pecked at his imagination.

"Are you a cop? Are you a detective? Going it alone. Not your best decision." The smugness in his partner's tone was to be expected, payback for the times Dennis had been the carrier of a similar missive. "What are we going to do about this mess?"

What are we going to do about this mess?

He ran the faces of his loved ones through his visual screen over and over, finally closing his eyes.

Raymond Parish is the pen name of a Midwestern writer, psychotherapist, and educator. He is the author of four critically praised non-fiction books and multiple non-fiction articles on subjects ranging from empowering cancer survivors to men in therapy. A love for mysteries and thrillers dating back to childhood inspired him to create the Hank Anderson fiction series. He lives in Missouri with his remarkable wife, his guitar, and his bicycle. Their amazing children, two daughters and a son, have launched.

Follow Raymond Parish, Thriller Author on Twitter @ParishAuthor

and

Goodreads

Made in the USA
Monee, IL
29 September 2022